New Ghost Stories IV

New Ghost Stories IV

The Fiction Desk Anthology Series
Volume Fifteen

Edited by Rob Redman

The Fiction Desk

ISBN 978-0-9927547-3-0

Please see our website for current contact
details and submissions information.

www.thefictiondesk.com

Printed and bound in the UK by Imprint Digital.

Contents

Introduction

Rob Redman

For a long time, these semi-regular anthologies of supernatural fiction happened almost by accident. We're lucky enough to see many great ghost stories among our submissions, and sometimes the quality and quantity taken together would suggest a dedicated anthology.

Now, having run a ghost story competition for several years (and since replaced it with an annual ghost story submission call, shifting the emphasis away from competitiveness and more towards variety), we can no longer realistically claim to have built this series-within-a-series in a fit of absent-mindedness. The joys of the supernatural in fiction are undeniable and, for us at least, unavoidable. (As, admittedly, are the joys of short stories that do not happen to feature the supernatural; for which see our previous anthology, or our next one.)

In the current volume we have ten superb authors whose work we would certainly recommend you neither deny nor avoid: Alastair Chisholm, Jo Gatford, Matt Plass, Cindy George, and Mark Taylor may be known to our regular readers from previous volumes, while Sarah Dale, Jacqueline Gabbitas, Gavin Eyers, Ben Tufnell, and Alan Gray are all making their first appearances in our pages. Among these writers are a gallery curator, a children's author, an Ethics and Compliance officer, an indeterminate number of journalists, and several psychologists.

Jo Gatford last appeared in our pages nine years ago, with her story 'Bing Bong' in There Was Once a Place. *Which makes her Fiction Desk stories rare as well as valuable. Like gold dust, in fact ...*

Yellow Rock

Jo Gatford

No one will say it out loud, but something strange is going on in Mine Number Eight. I count the faces as they emerge from the tunnel, name each man with a nod, one by one, to show them I'm not just counting cattle, but they don't even look up at me anymore. They don't care if I know who they are. All they know is it takes a day to replace them and the shift goes on regardless. All they know is that today they got to come back up.

The strangeness brings new faces faster than the east road. Before the rush, the town below the mountain was nothing but a lake and a scattering of bristlecone pines. Now it is a mud bowl full of hunger. An industrious purgatory through which a steady stream of men flows, exchanging glimmering hope for a pickaxe and a lantern and a train track into the bowels of a mountain. That a man would turn magpie and haul himself clear across the country to sift a river or tunnel through stone with his bare hands is oddity enough, but that is not what I mean.

The strangeness is down there, under the rock. Inside the earth. It fiddles with a person's thinking. Messes with my numbers. And I will swear on anything that moves there's nothing wrong with my counting — that's why Mr Fallow gave me this job; 'fastidious' he called me — but I will also swear blind that three Tuesdays ago sixty-four men walked out of that hole when I know for a fact sixty-five walked in.

* * *

When the line tailed off I waited, watching that dark archway for the last figure to push through into the sunlight. I knew his name then, but it's gone now — as though someone reached into my ear and pulled it out like a loose thread. I'll admit I was irritated by his lateness at first. I had to mark off the early shift before the second shift could head on down, and there's nothing more unsatisfying than an unbalanced ledger. I tailed after the second-to-last man to catch him — to ask how far behind his buddy might be — but he shook my hand from his sleeve and told me in no gentle manner to recount; that no sane man would spend another minute in there if they weren't being paid to. Besides, he didn't know no one by the name I'd already half forgotten. And then he looked behind my shoulder, like there was something staring back at him as if it might want to eat him, or me, or us both. I felt it too. An itch of a presence, cold as a shadow. I thought it might be the missing man, but when I turned there was nobody there.

And since by then I couldn't quite recall the spelling of the absentee's name, or whether that was indeed his name at all, and looking back at my roll call from the morning it was a little unclear whether the mark I had taken to be a five might not actually be a four, taking into account there was certainly some sort of smudge or line crossing over it, which could of course have been an errant scratch of my pencil but could also mean that I did not in fact miscount but that I had simply misread my previous total, I decided not to press it further.

I would like to believe it was a mistake. I surely would.

And I didn't mean to bring it up again, but there have been others since.

Two more, on a Friday morning shift — a pair of brothers who were certainly memorable enough, given that they stood half a head above the rest, making them stoop so they were almost hunched by the end of a day's work — but when they didn't return from the tunnel not a single person could place their names.

They'd barely been here a week. New blood, travelled all the way from the east coast by ship, they said. I remember that part distinctly; overheard it in a bar in town the evening before they joined the crew. I signed them on myself — I'll swear it on my mother's coffin — but there is not a scribble to mark their names there now. And when I try to picture their faces there's nothing but a smear, like paint touched before it's dry; a coil of pipe smoke fading into the air.

I was fastidious about it this time. Checked through my records twice before I went asking around. Methodical, like a newspaper man hustling up a story, or a lawyer cross-questioning a witness — both vocations that would have suited me far better than an accounts man, I think, though it's far too late for those kinds of ideas now, and I'm not too prideful to admit I was drawn here by the same longing as the rest of them. The same glowing yellow eye that led me into the mouth of the beast. And just because I work above ground and they toil beneath doesn't mean I haven't hung my life on the same damn nail.

Still. The workers don't like it when I come into the mess tent. They think I'm spying for the foreman; think I'm tallying up their break time and marking it against their pay. But for once I didn't bother about the glaring and the muttering. I asked them straight, one by one, where the brothers had gone. At first, they were irritated, as though I were some giant fly that had landed on the lip of their soup bowl, but I could see it in their eyes that they knew what I meant — who I meant — even if their tongues couldn't find the right names to describe them and their brains wouldn't admit the lost men were ever real. After a while, their irritation bled into a confusion that itched away at them, the same way it itched at me — a mere whisper below panic — and they became angry, or silent, or frightened, or a mixture of the three. No matter which, they waved me away all the same. So much easier to believe the impossible is just that.

Maybe they struck out before the shift, said one. *Wouldn't be the first to up and leave once they realised they'd bought shares in the pits of hell.*

The room undulated with agreeable nods, relieved that someone had offered a sensible explanation.

Or maybe Abacus just counted wrong, said another, and laughter echoed after my nickname, all the way out of the tent.

I didn't tell Mr Fallow. I'm not proud of it, but technically it wasn't as if I'd made any traceable errors and anyway, how could anybody contradict me when none of us could even remember what colour hair the missing men had on their heads? Think on this, I told myself: If they never existed in the first place, who's to miss them? It doesn't matter to Mr Fallow what names match which faces, so long as there are more than sixty men inside the mine on each rotation. And besides, it's not my job to ask questions. Questions only lead to more confusion. More mess. And I can't abide that.

The anonymous brothers made three. A week later there were seven. Or weren't seven. Were never seven. Two more after that made nine by Sunday. The half-built shack church down in the town tolled out at midday and the men flinched, shivering even in the sunshine, sidling looks at one another as if to wonder who might be next. If it might be them. I have tried to keep a tally of the ones that dropped off my ledger, but it's hard to keep count when the numbers won't stick and my hands tremble with the charcoal. Even when I'm sure I'm right, the marks seem to shift between blinks.

It unsettles us all. The absences we cannot see. There are spaces in the line that won't close. In the daytime we keep to the clock — shift in, shift out — and every evening I make up the deficit in town. There is no shortage of hungry eyes looking for an opening. I give them Mr Fallow's speech about the promise of prosperity and the rewards of hard work and I take down their names in my notebook and I watch visions of yellow rock circle above their heads like crows over carrion. Back at the camp I lay in my bunk and stare holes through the canvas above, imagining the yawning throat of the tunnel pulling me in and long-limbed shadow figures clutching at me, calling out in elongated vowels because they too have forgotten their names. Muted cries ripple through the night as though we are all sharing one nightmare.

Even Mr Fallow has noticed something is amiss, but his eyes still slide across the page when he asks to see the records. He checks the tally and nods and frowns and nods again and tells me I'm doing fine work, fine work, and we should be proud — Mine Number Eight is the most bountiful of all. On paper it's true, but I don't tell him what it's costing.

The men don't talk to me anymore. Barely even look up from the ground when they come back from below. I do my job, nonetheless. I count the faces, mark them off, tuck their names under my tongue and try to figure which ones are left unsaid; try to remember what I've forgotten. I've stopped looking at the scribbles on the page. They lie. They move. They are alive.

* * *

It happened again today. You can feel it coming. There's a tightening of the air, the way it closes in before a summer rainstorm — a crawling pressure that makes the thunderbugs curl and twitch. The men filed past with the pit in their eyes, and a knowing dread dripped down my spine like tar. A breeze nudged at my ledger and the numbers flickered. I tried to correct them, but a soot-blackened hand grabbed hold of my arm and my pencil scraped across the tally.

I looked up into the dish-white face of a man who spent more hours under the ground than over it. His fingers spidered at my wrist, as if unsure whether he wanted to embrace or shake me.

You've got to put a stop to this, Abacus, he hushed, his voice just as divided. *That boy. He was only seventeen.*

The same question I'd been asking for weeks lay dull in my stomach like dirt coffee. Burned as it rose in my throat. I swallowed it down. Asked anyway: *Who? What boy?*

The man shook his head, jostled me along with it, mouth stretched halfway between a grimace and a grin. An answer that caused him pain: *I don't know.*

I knew that one well enough. I pulled against his grip but my soul wasn't in it and he only held on tighter.

I don't know, the man said again, but I remember the whites of his eyes shining in the dark when he took his first track down. I remember him humming to keep from panicking. I remember that boy, even if I can't tell you his name.

I looked down at my list but I knew I wouldn't find it there either. This morning's total had been sixty-two. I knew that to be as true as anything I could swear on, though even my mother's face has become bleary in my memory these days, and I can't recall enough of any bible passage to do much good praying. Sixty-two, as sure as the sky is blue. But when I looked again the two had turned angular — a flat-bottomed one with a diagonal flick of a roof instead of a rounded curve.

Sixty-one then. In black and white. I was past the point of blinking at it.

It's no good, I told the man, holding up the nonsense ledger. *I can't prove anything.*

(And I am afraid.)

I still don't know if I said that part out loud but he reacted as if I did. Recoiled with a curling lip.

You could prove it, he said, *if you went down there and saw what we've seen. If you wrote it down. Fallow trusts what you've got in your notebook.*

A few heads flinched upward as they passed, but none looked me full in the eyes. I knew what they thought of me. A cattle-counting money man with one hand in Fallow's pocket and the other on the scales; one eye on my tallies, the other on the clock. But at least I'd tried. I'd done my best to make the numbers match, and untangle the names from my tongue. And what had they done? Laughed at me and called me names.

I plucked my shirtsleeve out of the man's fist and ushered him back to the line with a sweep of my pencil. He stopped after two paces and stared straight at my naked fear like gravy on my shirt front. This time his voice was a rasp of boot track on packed earth.

We're all afraid, he said. *Every one of us. Every damn time the shift bell rings.*

He spat in the dust at my feet. It was thick and black. I watched it sink into the thirsty desert and disappear.

Go and see, he said again, and though he barely whispered it had the force of sixty-one men behind it.

* * *

Someone has left a lamp by the doorway.

I take up my book and pencil and I don't look back to see if they are watching, even when the sound of the mess tent dies to a flutter. I wait for laughter that does not come. That I had hoped would come. All of it an elaborate prank on old Abacus. But there is nothing but the creaking of the winches and the sift of wind on sand.

The mouth of the tunnel welcomes me like shade on a searing day. I imagined walking into the darkness would be like passing through a curtain but it is a gradual blinding. You only realise the light has truly gone when your eyes start aching with the effort of pushing forward. The glow of the lantern is a small and choking comfort as the air turns cold and dead and motionless, chilling the sweat on my back.

The seams don't start for a mile and a half – I know that much from Mr Fallow's records, even if I've never set foot down here. A short walk for any able-bodied man, no matter whether he uses a pickaxe or a pen. A mile and a half in and a quarter mile down, not that you'd notice the gradient unless you're going upward. I hope I'll get to climb back up, though I don't much like the idea of having to turn my back on the maw. At least going down I can face whatever is waiting for me head on.

I keep to the middle of the tunnel – the jagged rock on either side is slick with a moisture that smells of stale, buried things – but the tracks trip my steps and the walls offer no steadying hold, only bloody palms and a chill that bites to the bone. Soon the rails are my only view, forward or back, and the dark presses in, filling the tunnel with its heaviness – such a large, tangible thing you could almost put a hand out to touch it. The sound of my own footsteps becomes a heartbeat.

The scrabbling of rodents and the clicking echoes of bats splinter my sense of direction into pieces. From below there comes the sing of metal, pure as a pebble dropped into a pond. The rumble of men's voices spirals up and away again, like a phonograph wound too tight. The stink of copper rises from the mud at my feet.

I almost turn back, I'm not ashamed to say. It is my shame that brought me here. The invisible tally I signed my name to. And I remember that boy too, even if I didn't admit it before. I remember him: only seventeen and more afraid than any of us. Only here because they are running out of men down in the town; because he knew no better and hadn't heard the rumours about Mine Number Eight; because Fallow twisted his ear. Or maybe it was me. I lose track now.

But I remember him and that is something. And I will not turn back until whatever is down here has weighed my soul. My feet move without orders and the voices thin until I can hear only one. Calling for me.

Abacus.

Not my real name but I have forgotten the one I was born with.

Abacus, come and see.

And just when I think I can't bear to see another inch of black, lonely rock, there it shines: a slice of yellow like a snake swimming inside the mountain wall, stretching down deep into the below, singing *follow, follow,* sweet as a choir boy. The craving is a hook in my gut, drawing me towards the glimmer and the warmth, towards a crack in the stone where a trickle of gold provides the only light for miles. Maybe the only light left in the whole world. Maybe above ground there is only darkness now. Maybe this is all there is.

And I see.

The hook twists, turning me ravenous, and I tear at the edges of the seam with my hands. It shouldn't be possible, not without a pick and hours of labour, but the rock crumbles beneath my fingers like clay and the crack cleaves wide to let me in, as though it has been waiting for me all this time; has been hankering, just as I have. And I feel the balance shift. I remember every name of every man the mountain has ever taken and I know now that there is another, second tally — one I have failed to see all this time — and finally the numbers make sense.

I go willingly. Sink into molten yellow, limbless and formless and satiate at last.

* * *

The next shift finds my broken lantern a mile and a half in, a quarter mile down. I hear them remark on the spill of oil, but none ponders further to question whose it might have been. They glance at the seam on the wall — a streak of life within the stone — but their hunger frightens them and they cannot look for long. They do not see the whites of my eyes. They do not hear me calling. They do not remember me except as a buzzing inside their skulls. They huddle with their coffee cans and long for sunlight. They tell themselves the yellow rock is worth it.

A *fair exchange*, the mountain thinks. And, if I had my pocket book and pencil and fingers to write with, I would be inclined to agree.

Book lovers will already know that surrounding yourself
with the written word places you at the centre of an ongoing
conversation – and that's especially true in the following story.

Years Together

Alan Gray

He'd been a latecomer to love, but at thirty-five he was confident
that love was what he had with Hannah. She was his longest
relationship (three years on his previous), and he was older
now, he knew how to make things work.

Like tonight, for instance, he had hoovered the flat
and cooked dinner. He'd even gone to the trouble of
buying candles and lighting them for the occasion. It was
sentimental but it would please her, and besides – it was
their anniversary.

He poured the shells of pasta into the boiling water and
sipped his glass of wine. A playlist muffled the kitchen's
silence and distracted him from the discovery he had made
earlier.

He chopped the tomatoes and tried not to think; rinsed the
chopping board, prepared the basil.

Emma, his ex, used to write notes (or rather, semi-poems) on little scraps of paper and he'd found one whilst cleaning, buried behind a potted plant. A wadded snippet covered in dust and dirt. The ink splotched by the damp. It was her handwriting, he'd recognised the spiky block letters:

For where it has once appeared, it longs to appear
again.

When Hannah had first moved in, she would find this sort of thing everywhere. Tucked into the back of a cupboard, underneath the TV stand, slotted into books and scrawled across pages. At first, she'd been disturbed — unnerved by the whole thing — but then she'd grown used to it. Accepting in her dark, sophisticated way that 'everybody has their baggage'.

Hannah would joke about the notes mostly, and he'd try to laugh along, relieved she was able to see the funny side. But every now and then cold thoughts would rise up. A pang of — well, he wasn't sure. He would smile and his throat would tighten. He would smile and his lips would stiffen and crack.

'Your ex-girlfriend wants to speak to you,' Hannah would say, holding the note aloft and at a distance, as if she were afraid of infection. 'She's here in the kitchen'; 'here in the living room'; 'behind the bed' ...

Once, he'd turned from the book he was reading to see Hannah wryly brandishing another scrap of paper. Her intelligent eyes widened with mock horror, her bobbed brown hair framing her face.

'Found herself a good spot in the spice rack,' she'd said, shaking the pot she held in her other hand. 'I guess you don't like turmeric.'

He'd paused, considering how to respond.

'I wouldn't care,' Hannah said, turning the note over between her fingers. 'Just last week I spoke to her at the bottom of the recycling bin.'

* * *

Hannah was going to be late and the pasta was already overcooked. He'd been stupid enough to put it on before she arrived, and now he was going to have to eat it himself. Leaving the best of it in Tupperware.

'I'm really sorry,' she had said, when she'd called him moments earlier, obviously in a hurry. 'There's salmon in the fridge, you should help yourself.'

He'd played it down. He'd missed far too many of their anniversaries to have argued his case. Though as the call went on, he heard what he took to be the fuzzy background noise of some kind of party or bar. The distant murmuring of indistinct chatter.

'Where are you?' he said, and a rustling fell on the line, as if she were cupping the receiver.

'In the office,' she said. 'It's a nightmare. There's just so much to do.'

He waited — as if to give her a chance to say more.

'We can do something at the weekend,' he said, and she said, 'Yeah, maybe.'

Then she laughed and said, 'it's not like you're alone. Sassy will look after you. Just make sure you feed her.'

The dog looked up at him expectantly.

* * *

He helped himself now, not to the salmon in the fridge but to the pasta dish — which he ate at the table, reluctant to blow out the candles and neglect the waiting cutlery. He threw some pasta at Sassy's feet and watched her eat it. She wasn't supposed to eat 'human food', and certainly not from the floor, but it was something he enjoyed watching. The speed with which she ate anything put before her — the way she licked the laminate clean, then licked her paws for good measure.

He poured himself another glass of wine, and stared at the empty chair facing him. The music whispered soothingly about love and loss, heartbreak and heartbreakers.

He turned it off, preferring to sit in silence.

> *The world is weary of me,*
> *And I am weary of it*

That was what Hannah had found that time in the spice rack.

It was a quote from Charles D'Orleans. A mediaeval poet Emma must've encountered in some random anthology, the kind she'd regularly buy from charity shops. Two for a pound.

Was it how she felt? Was it how she wanted him to feel?

He'd thrown the present note away, but now he removed it from the bin and considered it in detail, as if the handwriting itself possessed some essential meaning. A hidden clue.

> *For where it has once appeared, it longs to appear*
> *again.*

He laughed. And returned it scrunched to the bin.

* * *

'I think she's haunting you,' Hannah had said, when she'd discovered a little pink card of Emma's about three years into their relationship. At that point they hadn't seen any of her 'letters' in some time and the joke had gone dry.

'Please,' he'd said, 'let's just forget about it.' But the idea that she was haunting him had stuck.

He'd searched for her on Facebook and found nothing. Googled her, checked the website of the local paper, and still came up empty.

'Maybe she's got something to hide,' his friends had said. But he doubted that. She just didn't care much for technology, never had.

There were times he wondered if the notes fitted together in some way. Though he'd chucked out most of them to avoid upsetting Hannah — and his memory was vague at best.

Occasionally a forgotten note would enter his mind and mingle with others that resided there:

Night shows something hopeless —

— which consciousness unravels to reach

For the eye altering alters all

And then it'd be lost again, as if the text were too faint to read, jumbled like that of a dream.

The memory would still be there, but it would be inaccessible — stowed away somewhere until the most trivial thing would bring it to mind. The way the foam formed atop his morning coffee (*'Behold therein a hundred seas displayed'*); the grim sound of a passing night bus (*'Time had been moving on wings of lead'*); his awful reflection in a computer monitor ('*There is no God but this mirror that thou seest*') —

It was as if she were communicating with him, commenting on his life.

'Where do you think she is now?' Hannah had once asked, and though he strongly suspected Emma had gone back to the small town where they'd first met, a twist in his stomach told him otherwise.

Dead, he thought. And for some reason he believed it.

* * *

He knew he didn't deserve the life he had now. The walks in the park; the cuddles on the sofa; the kisses when they parted for work in the morning and when they reunited at night.

He didn't deserve any of it.

Of course, Hannah had told him otherwise. But she didn't know the details, the type of person he'd been before they met; the way he'd used people — used Emma. It wasn't just that he'd cheated on her, though he had, several times over. It was more that he'd never loved her, never even tried. She had been temporary to him, nothing more; and yet the relationship had gone on for years — filling with lies and deceit, eating away at her trust for people, the reliability of her own mind.

Emma had been smart, but he'd discouraged her from studying. She'd had money, but he had wasted it. She'd loved him, and he'd treated her like shit.

They had planned to have a baby together. Babies even. But instead he'd kicked her out, made all kinds of threats.

'You don't understand,' she'd said, that night in the living room, wailing. 'You don't understand anything'.

She turned to him and her face seemed to age in the lamplight. Her skin, pale and almost transparent: the veins in her hands and arms suggesting themselves, their gentle blue.

'You never have done,' she continued, fists blanching, 'and never will.'

She'd left for good after that: not even sticking around to gather her belongings. The books and notepads she'd accumulated, the clothes she used to pile on the floor.

Nobody knew where she'd gone. Most people he knew didn't know much about her at all. Nothing had been said and nobody had had the chance to ask.

She'd moved to the city to stay with him — away from her family and friends.

'It's where my job is,' he'd told her many times over. 'It's not like we can live anywhere else.'

* * *

In the silence, his fork clanked against the plate and he took another bite. He wasn't a good cook, but it had come out better than expected. He'd obviously learned a few tricks from Hannah, serving as her sous-chef, and it saddened him she wasn't here to witness this fact.

'*In the end, we are all of us alone,*' he thought, recalling another snippet — and he remembered Hannah accusing him of writing the notes himself.

'Ghosts can't write,' she'd said, half-smilingly, on one of their date nights, and he'd considered the idea that the whole thing was some kind of unconscious prank. That maybe he was both victim and perpetrator.

He looked again at the empty chair in front of him and felt the table shiver and vibrate.

His phone was ringing. Hannah.

He answered it, and the other end gave no response.

'Hannah?' he said, and Sassy looked up at him. 'Hello?' he said.

The line was bad — dreadful — and his own voice echoed and echoed.

'Hannah?' he repeated, and he felt like he was opening a very large door and inviting something in.

* * *

He drank the last of the wine and drew himself a bath. The flat had grown large and cold in Hannah's absence, and containing himself in hot water seemed like the most immediate solution.

He'd bought Hannah several bath bombs earlier that week — a nest of them — and he used one for himself now. Feeling the loss of three pounds as he watched it fizzle and melt.

'The bath is where we tell each other secrets,' Hannah had once said. But mostly they'd just fucked in there. The bath was big: it was only inevitable they would take advantage. And besides, was he really complaining? Tonight he'd thought more fucking was in store — a good deal more. But the tub filled up around him, and the water changed to greenish-blue, and he felt himself flinch as it lapped up against the top of his chest and arms. Trickling like the light touch of caressing fingers.

He dipped his head under the water and closed his eyes. The sound of the rushing tap filled the hot, bubbling world below. He turned it off with his foot, and listened as all fell still and silent.

An anniversary for one, he thought, and wondered, melodramatically, what gift was associated with being together for five years —

Wood. The material of coffins.
Daisies. The flowers pushing up.

* * *

On their second anniversary (paper / lily of the valley), he'd been doing overtime at work and had found one of Emma's notes tucked away in a drawer. She must have slotted it into one of his folders at some point and it had slipped out and found itself beneath a long-abandoned box of breakfast bars. The note was torn, ripped from a ring-binder and covered in grid lines.

The message:

> No space of regret can make amends for one life's opportunity misused.

It was a quote from Charles Dickens, whom she'd been reading the Christmas before they'd broken up. Part of her plan to better herself — her vague attempt to become somebody different.

She'd got books from the library, and he'd complained about them being everywhere, taking up too much room. But when Christmas came around, they'd read A Christmas Carol to one another and smoked weed on the couch. He'd been out of it, but this line had caught his attention. Enough at least to remember its source when he saw it again, alone in his empty office.

'Do you think we'll have two children or three?' Emma had said that night, staring at the wall with the spliff between her fingers. She turned to him and her expression flickered as her mind focused on him and the present moment. 'Because I always thought I'd have twins,' she continued. 'And, I don't know, I guess I always imagined having them first: the twins and then another one a few years later.'

* * *

The water had grown cold, and the bottle of wine sat empty on the side of the bath. He could easily drink another, but he wouldn't. He could easily do a lot of things he no longer did. But he won't.

The bathroom fan whirred indifferently. He shifted his position and the water gave a languorous, green-blue ripple.

'Maybe the messages are for me,' Hannah had said thoughtfully, lying in bed one night. 'Maybe she didn't like the idea of you moving on. Or maybe — maybe it was just some weird memory thing. Reminders for herself.'

He had wrapped his arm gently around her, and she'd begun to cry. He stroked her hair and she abruptly brushed his hand away.

'Just give me a minute,' she said, her voice coming at him from the black. 'I'll be okay in the morning. I promise.'

He imagined Hannah looking at her phone now and dismissing it. His name appearing and disappearing in her purse. A lighthouse in the dark sea of her life's clutter.

Is it possible that she is — ? he wondered. He didn't finish the thought: what he meant was undefinable.

* * *

Soon Hannah would arrive and he'd ask her where she'd been. He'd tell her about the pasta he'd cooked, and she'd open the fridge. A grim Tupperware box beside the salmon.

He'd want to ask her about work, about the background noise – about the party – but instead they'd kiss. Her cold body pressed to his, the damp city air still clinging to her coat.

'I love you,' she'd say, and he'd pause and say: 'I can't imagine being with anybody else.'

Hannah's eyes would become just a little bit paler. And he'd picture a distant family with many children.

*Music and the supernatural are both regular themes in our anthologies,
so it's always a pleasure to have the two combined in one story.
Without further ado, therefore, I'll hand you over to Ben Tufnell ...*

An Invocation

Ben Tufnell

Can I get a red wine, darling?

Thanks. Okay, shall we start?

Right, good evening. It's an honour to be invited to speak here
today. I don't usually find myself in such esteemed surroundings.
I'm going to be talking about a photograph I took of the great
James Dee in 1973, shortly before his untimely demise. Or rather,
I should say, his untimely disappearance. Maybe he's still out there
somewhere. Let's hope so.

Here it is, on the screen behind me.

Not bad, is it?

It's my most reproduced photograph. Someone once said it was
on the wall of a million teenage bedrooms, which is a humbling
thought. I'm supposed to say something about how I made it and
why I think it's a successful photograph and why it has had the
impact it has. We'll get on to that. But first I'll give you some context.

The band was at the peak of their powers. They'd just released their third album, *Voodoo Mother, Demon Brother,* and it was clearly something very special. Without compromising their vision in the slightest, they had somehow nailed the crossover. They were on what would have been their last tour of what we might call mid-sized venues, the theatres and the Uni halls. After this it was going to be stadiums and arenas. America. The big time. The very big time.

I'd met the band and photographed them a few times before, even right at the beginning, and I'd always found them good company. Down to earth, nice blokes. We'd enjoyed a few drinks together. Dee — Jim — and I got on okay. He was pretty intense company and saw himself as an 'artist', which of course he was. To be honest, I was closer to Nick and the others. The pleasures of the road and all that. You know what I'm saying. Anyway, this time round it was immediately clear something had changed. The atmosphere around them was dense. It was charged. And it wasn't just that everyone, from the management to the promotors to the road crew, knew that they were about to go supernova. No, it was something else. Hard to explain really. There was a heaviness.

I wondered if it was the drugs. Of course, later on there were the rumours of black magic and that absurd court case in the US. And all of that was encouraged by the weird circumstances around Dee's disappearance.

Anyway, by the time I hooked up with the tour he was *crackling.* Really, you had the feeling that if you touched him — and Jesus, a lot of people wanted to touch him — you would get an electric shock.

I was hired by the magazine to shoot three concerts towards the end of the tour: Birmingham, Manchester, and then the finale at the Royal Albert Hall. They were going to do a big special. Cover feature, interview with Jim, review of the tour, and so on. Usually for those jobs I had one night and would roam around and take pictures from different places. Play it by ear, find the good angles. Every venue is different and every performance is new so you have to react. But this time, I thought I would be very disciplined and focus on one position each evening. I had an inkling that they were building to something special for the final night and so I thought I would save the pit photos for then. That's the position you tend to get the best head shots from, the close ups.

The Birmingham gig was good. Really good. I remembered then what a great band they were live. I was at the side of the stage and I took about five rolls while they were on stage. Then another roll backstage in the dressing rooms. I thought I had some good shots but afterwards, when I developed the films, about half of them were blank. And the others were ruined by these weird flares and burns, a bit like you get when film is exposed to radiation. Couldn't explain it. Faulty film, perhaps. Very odd.

The second night I was concentrating on what I call the big picture shots: the whole stage, the band in full flight, the light show. Wide angle. Management got me access to one of the opera boxes up and to the side, and I got some great angles looking down from there, and then went down and was taking views from the side of the stage and through the backline and drum kit: the band, their backs to me, and the sea of faces beyond. The unholy congregation. The sense of devotion, of worship even, was incredible. But then the strap on my camera snapped and the case cracked open on the floor, exposing the film. I started to feel the job was cursed. Of course, I had a couple of cameras, all with different lenses, but that was the one I thought had the best shots. It was a strange accident. Never happened before and never happened since. At the end I had some okay images from that night but nothing of the individual members of the band. So the pressure was on me for the finale at the Royal Albert Hall.

On the day the sense of expectation was massive. When I arrived to check out the venue and the angles — this was hours before they opened the doors — there were huge crowds outside already. Some of the kids had gone over the road into Hyde Park and had lit fires. There were police. You could feel the tension and anticipation. You just knew it was going to be one of those seminal gigs. You know, one of the ones that everyone says they were at.

When they came on it was clear they wanted to make a statement. Given my run of bad luck I was super careful with my kit and hoped I would get some good pictures.

They were brilliant. Committed, tight, electric. The climax of the gig was a massive version of 'Maelstrom'. Everyone knows that track now; the single is one of those classics that you find on pub jukeboxes and even hear on drivetime radio shows. But that version is heavily edited compared to the album track, and live it was a very different beast again.

In the middle section, which even on the album version has just a short guitar solo, they would do something very different. There is a descending sequence of chords, down through the octave alternating majors and minors, hitting the so-called Devil's Interval, the *Diabolus in Musica*, the tritone, the unholy flatted fifth, and then at the bottom of the octave looping round again, so that it feels as if the descent goes on and on, down and down and down. And at that time, when they did it live, they would lock into that loop and just keep going. No solos. Just layers of noise, building. It was incredible. Very very heavy. It just went on and on. And when you thought that surely it had gone on too long and they were about to break back into the chorus, it would go on even more and if anything would have even more intensity and volume. Nick, Johnny, and Mac would be locked into their groove, at the back of the stage by the drum riser, all with their heads down. In the zone. And James Dee would go into full shaman mode, dancing, whirling, exhorting the front rows of the audience and gesturing deep into the darkness of the auditorium, pulling the audience to come unto himself. Great stuff. Magnetic. Powerful.

The audience would go nuts and the lighting guy would throw everything at it, strobes and so on, which made it a nightmare for me. With the lights and the dry ice and everything else it was almost impossible to see what I was shooting so I just pointed and clicked and hoped for the best. You may laugh, but it's the truth. We don't always know what we're doing.

There's a lot of luck in photography.

So we were in the maelstrom, descending and descending, on a wild helter-skelter ride, heading into the heart of darkness, and Dee was spinning in the centre of the stage like a dervish. Spinning and spinning. And it seemed to me there was a darkness there, a gathering of density around him. And I swear I saw flames. I thought it was part of the show but afterwards the manager, who had seen them too, said it wasn't. But the stage was definitely scorched. There were burn marks, like someone had kindled a campfire right there on the stage. The roadcrew puzzled over that later on when they dismantled everything.

Well, that's the story. Let's take a look at the image. Of course it has been so popular because of the expression on his face. That's why it's been so successful as a poster. Look at him. Handsome devil.

We can talk about film stock and printing and so on but I can't really say anything about the technical aspect of the shoot, f-stops and exposures and all that. Shooting in that situation is very intuitive. In the moment, when it's happening, I'm really just improvising. And at that moment, like I said, with the strobes and smoke bombs and everything, I was almost shooting blind. They say you make your own luck, and on that night I was obviously lucky. The framing is perfect, even if I say so myself. I didn't have to crop at all when it came to the printing.

But what I think is so extraordinary is this. Here. Can you see? The second figure? Must be eight feet tall. I'm always surprised by how many people don't see it. Of course, once you've seen it you can't unsee it. But is it just a glitch in the image, shadows and light and reflections, or was he really there? I don't know, I really don't.

But I do know something in the air changed as the music spiralled down into the depths. We all felt it. And honestly, for a moment there, I felt absolutely terrified. I was in the presence of something I couldn't really see but which I could definitely feel. Maybe it was just the music, or maybe not. Whatever it was, it was awesome. I've spoken to a few people who were there, both crew and kids who were in the audience, and we all felt the same thing. It was like something entered the building. For a moment I saw the darkness forming and clinging to Jim, like smoke, wrapping around him like a shroud. And his face, I could see that he was terrified too. You know when you're on a roller coaster and the penny drops that it is going to be way more scary than you thought? It was like that. Of course, in the picture, it looks like he is in ecstasy. Photographs can lie.

And of course, there were other photographers there that night and other pictures. But this is the only one where you can see that second figure.

It was a hell of a concert. 'Maelstrom' seemed to go on for hours and it was amazing. Like being hit by a truck. The sound was at eleven, for sure. When they brought it to a close it was like the venue had been turned upside down by an earthquake. When the sound stopped there was a moment of silence and it was like a vacuum, like the air had been sucked out of the space.

The audience were broken. But they were still calling for more.

Normally, the band would come back on for an encore (they usually did 'Possession' and a really early song like 'Nerve Endings'), but that night it just wasn't possible. They had given everything. There was a weird stillness. I looked back out into the crowd and saw that half a dozen people had passed out. Others were literally on their knees, weeping. As the smoke began to clear, the lighting guy put up the lights on the crowd and turned off the lights on the stage. It was the end.

Backstage, in the dressing rooms, Dee was already locked away and wouldn't see anyone. He'd come off stage in a real state apparently. The stage manager said he looked haunted. That was his exact word: *haunted*. The others were in a state of shock. Later, Nick told me he'd felt something pass through them. He'd felt that something had been released. And because of that he was working on a bottle of Scotch and a massive reefer. To bring himself down, as he said. Johnny kept on saying he needed oxygen. More air, more air. Mac was out cold on the floor in a corner.

We all know what happened next.

I never saw James Dee again. And incredibly, it seems this is actually the last picture ever taken of him. When, after he had gone, the band decided to do a 'best of' album, they used my image on the cover. And that was that. A million bedrooms.

So, any questions?

Living in a shared house has its challenges at the best of times, and as Gavin Eyers shows in his first Fiction Desk story, things don't get any easier when only one of you is actually living at all.

Here Too

Gavin Eyers

When I walked up the pathway with the estate agent that summer's day, and stepped over the threshold for the first time, you were watching me, weren't you?

I was too distracted to realise, as I admired the ivy that crept over the old brick walls and the tall chimneys, as I explored the many rooms. I liked the sweeping staircase and the big attic where spiders had spun webs around an empty antique chest of drawers. I listened while the estate agent pointed out original features: the boot scraper, ceiling roses, fireplaces. It was a house from the past; too old-fashioned for my usual tastes, but somehow I felt as though I'd just come home.

I like to think that you gave me those peaceful first few days after I moved in because you knew how much I appreciated the house, though, in truth, I don't know your reason. You were dormant as I unpacked boxes and began to arrange things. I went from room to room and imagined what the place might look like once I was settled, considered where I might place a bookcase or hang a painting. I was quite lost with all the space — some rooms were totally bare. I had plenty of choice as to where I should put my bed. One room I turned into a gym with my bench and weights. Sometimes, I just sat and appreciated the quietness, the house smelling of time and faintly of wood.

Then one night, you made yourself known to me. I was woken in the dark by creaking floorboards. You had me wandering the landings in my boxers, searching for intruders.

The following night you slammed a door, then rattled a window. I kept the lights on until morning.

After that I began to ponder this house, to absorb it, and I realised that my new home was a place of subtle, unanswered questions: in the corner of the garden shed were a few rusty tools — to whom did they belong? Who once looked at themselves and straightened their tie, or brushed their hair, in the oval mirror in the rear box bedroom? The chest of drawers in the attic — in which year did it cease to be used, and who hauled it up that staircase?

This house is so very old.

And there were other traces of other times here, too: in the living room was the smell of a coal bucket that wasn't there, in one of the bedrooms a hint of perfume, and in the empty study was the unmistakeable scent of old books. Impossible echoes linger here.

I had lived in this house for only a few weeks before you started interfering with my belongings. Things were not always where I'd left them. My toothbrush was inexplicably in the toilet bowl. My baseball cap went missing. One morning, as I was about to go jogging, I found that the laces on my trainers were tied together.

You knew all the tricks.

Did they work, those games, to move on others who'd lived here before me? Was that why this massive house was within my budget? You soon found out that although I scare easily, I am stubborn. We have something in common, you and I.

So you upped your game.

Instead of rattling windows, you rattled my bed violently, waking me in the night, soaked in my own sweat. You threw things across rooms that smashed into tiny pieces. You scrawled big, indecipherable messages onto walls and as I grabbed my phone to take a picture, you erased them. When I had mates over for matches on TV or drunken nights listening to music, you behaved perfectly and I knew that I should speak of you to no one, in case they didn't believe me.

I wondered how I might rid the house of you, to have this place to myself, but one day, I calmed down and began to think: who am I to say that someone else doesn't belong here? I decided there had been enough of this nonsense and that we should try to live together here, to share the house. It was right then, as I stood in the kitchen on a bright and sunny afternoon, that from somewhere upstairs I heard a bang. I found my way to the attic, to the chest of drawers that I'd seen there before and *yes*, I thought, *that was it* – the sound of a drawer being slammed shut.

That night I was woken by what sounded like the chest of drawers being dragged, agonisingly loudly, across the floor of the attic, over and over again. I was too frightened to investigate. I just sat up in bed and stared at the ceiling, astounded at your power.

The next morning I crept up the stairs and found the drawers precisely where they should have been, and it really unsettled me. Then I opened a drawer. It was empty, just as before, but when I was closing it, I saw something almost out of sight at the back. It was an old sepia photograph, the size of a playing card, and there you were.

You are a woman.

For your photograph you wore a high-collared white blouse and a dark billowing skirt, and your dark hair was tied back. You are older than me. You are beautiful, and you had a stern expression as you stood at the front gate with this great house behind you. I turned the picture over, hoping for an inscription, but there was nothing.

I took you downstairs and rested you on the mantel. I got my tool box. Near the foot of the staircase, halfway up the wall, I drilled a hole and placed a screw. I searched for a frame that I'd bought years before; second hand and rustic, made from strong wood. I knew that it'd be perfect for you.

I hung your photo there at the foot of the stairs, the heart of the house, so that you can see the comings and goings with your paper eyes. Your little image dominates the big wall, draws people to look at you. When visitors ask who you are, I tell them that you once lived here. I don't tell them that you still live here. I don't think you want me to, do you?

So now, we share.

It's been a while since I moved in. My food is in the kitchen cupboards, my beer in the fridge. My music sounds throughout the house. My dirty clothes are in the wash bin, my razor is beside the sink. I'm at home here, and I love this house. I know that you love this house, too.

But, you have got me thinking. Will I one day creep along the landings as you do? Will I lurk at the edge of the next resident's vision, only to disappear when they turn their head? Will I make the floorboards creak, forget to close doors quietly, and move the belongings of others; simply because things are not where they should be?

I've heard less from you lately, though I know you're still here. My possessions are mostly untouched, but I know that you watch me.

Sometimes I stop and look at your photograph at the foot of the stairs and feel pity for your unquiet soul. One night, I lit a candle for you and left it on the mantel, but you blew it out.

As every child knows, darkness is so much more than simply the absence of light. And as Sarah Dale's story reminds us, some family secrets are buried so deep in the darkness that no light will ever reach them.

Not After Midnight

Sarah Dale

Brady points the torch upwards under his chin.

'Fancy a game of Blair Witch?'

I smile, but my breathing is too fast. I take a deeper breath and straighten my shoulders.

'How long do you think the battery'll last?' I say.

'No idea. Have we got any more anywhere?'

'Your guess is as good as mine.'

Brady found the torch in a drawer full of odds and ends. Perished elastic bands, shoelaces, a screwdriver, a tiny tape measure that looks as if it came out of a cracker. He rummages through it again.

'Can't find any.'

The wind roars around the house. The old chimney, blocked where it would once have serviced a kitchen range, echoes and amplifies it. I am put in mind of the three little pigs. We used to have a picture book of that story. I wonder if it is still in the house somewhere.

The October storm has knocked the power out to the whole village. As if in emphasis, the torch bulb flickers. Its weak light goes out.

'Damn,' Brady says. 'What are we going to do now?'

'Help me look for candles. You know what Granny was like, there must be some here somewhere.'

We fumble through cupboards and drawers. Bang into things.

'Hurrah,' Brady eventually announces, triumphant. 'Birthday cake candles!'

There are loads of them, mostly half used, packed into old tobacco tins. Brady surprises me and pulls a lighter from his pocket. I wonder when and why he's started smoking again, but I don't say anything.

We peer at each other in the weirdly festive light. The chances of a tree coming down in the lane between us and the pub seem high enough for neither of us to want to venture out tonight. We'll have to make do with the few things we brought with us. I pass him an apple.

'Did you like coming here when we were kids?' Brady asks.

'Sort of. I was always excited, but nervous too. I used to bring toys to make myself feel braver. It was all the old stuff that scared me. Grandad's shoes and coat still in the cupboard under the stairs. So ghostly. That creepy huge figurehead in the shed.'

Everyone who ever lived here is dead now. Finally, we are the grown-ups. Brady looks as much at a loss as I feel. We don't know how to be newly orphaned in our fifties. It feels ridiculous.

'I never liked coming,' he says. 'How come Mum and Dad didn't sell this place when Granny died?'

'I don't know. They came down a couple of times a year to check things over. Mum used to say she wished someone local lived here but she never did anything about it. Wouldn't talk about it apart from once when she said something I didn't understand about not wishing it on anyone. Clammed up after that.'

Granny — our mother's mother — lived her whole life here. It is dark and musty. It has no central heating. It's been left as Granny left it. There is a pantry, with gauze at the air vent and mesh covers for cheese and cakes. We find a storm lantern there, with oil still in it, and to our surprise it lights easily.

Our spirits raised, we light a fire in the living room grate. The wind keeps blowing the smoke back at us, in huge billowing waves. My eyes stream. The fire takes ages to start drawing adequately and when it starts to give out some heat, we decide to sleep in the living room. There's still no power, and the bedrooms feel dismal and cold. I congratulate myself on remembering to bring air beds from home.

'Do you realise we probably haven't shared a room for about forty years?' I say, stretching into the comforting dry warmth of my sleeping bag. It smells like my house. We raise glasses of whiskey to each other, having found half a bottle of Jameson in the sideboard. I feel like a survivor of something, as we watch the shadows vaulting round the room.

'Pains me to admit it, Sis, but I'm glad you're here,' says Brady. 'What with the racket outside and the way the shadow looks like a person up that wall there, I could be a bit freaked out on my own.'

I laugh.

'By the way, that *is* a shadow of a person. It's me, can't you see? But you're right. The noise alone is enough to give me the heebie-jeebies.'

Rain — or maybe hail — starts to shell the windows. Branches scrape back and forth, screeching against the old glass, and I can hear the wind reverberating steadily way up in the sky above the house.

'Do you hear the sea?' I say. 'Listen — it's that booming noise. Granny always said if you could hear it from here, it was the signal for people to go out wrecking once the tide was out. I think that's where half of the stuff in the cupboards came from. Grandad probably had something to do with it all.'

We lie in the darkness, listening hard.

'Oh, okay. Now I'm starting to imagine things,' Brady says. 'You're going to have to keep chatting before I convince myself there are babies crying upstairs, and somebody whistling in the garden.'

I laugh and sit up to pour more whiskey into our glasses.

'Hang on, what's the time? Do you know?'

Brady's watch lights up as he looks.

'It's ten to twelve. Why?'

'I was just remembering how Granny and Mum were always so strict about us needing to be asleep — the lights *had* to be out — before midnight. Granny used to say that an hour of sleep before midnight was worth two after. Do you remember the time we wanted a midnight feast?'

Brady shakes his head.

'What happened?'

'Mum was so fierce. Eventually she let us have some biscuits in bed, but was so adamant — *not after midnight*, she kept saying. She and Granny kept reminding us. It wasn't much fun after all. They'd put us both off. I was convinced that something terrible would happen if we kept the light on beyond midnight here. We always went to bed early.'

'The lantern doesn't count,' Brady says, winking at me. 'We'll brave it out tonight.' We laugh, and change the subject, talking about our children and work until the unease in our voices fades. At last we sleep.

* * *

I wake after deep sleep to hear Brady poking the fire and talking about tea. There is still no power.

'What time is it?' I ask, running my hand through my hair.

'Sevenish,' he says. 'It'll be light soon.'

'God, that's too early.' I burrow into my sleeping bag. 'But tea would be good,' I shout through the opening. 'Maybe you can do it on the fire with a saucepan.'

I pretend to sleep whilst I listen to Brady crashing around. Eventually, he puts a mug of surprisingly good tea on the floor next to me. I sit up and cradle it.

'Is it still stormy?'

'Seems to have quietened down. I heard the church clock strike a while back. Still dark though. I guess it's all the vegetation. I'll have a look outside.'

When he comes back into the room, he's frowning.

'My watch says it's 8:07. But it's dark outside, as if it's the middle of the night.'

'What's your phone clock say?'

'It's out of charge. Where's yours?'

I grimace at him, feeling embarrassed.

'You won't believe this. I dropped it down the toilet last week. It's buggered. I haven't got a replacement yet. Reckoned I wouldn't need it down here anyway, there's never any signal.'

He laughed. 'You're worse than the kids.'

'At least I don't smoke.' Without waiting for a response, I say, 'I'll get up and head to the shop. We could fry bacon over the fire. The estate agent's due at eleven, you said?'

I dress in yesterday's clothes and roll up my sleeping bag. Drive to the village. There is no one about. The shop is shut even though the sign on the door says it opens at eight, and it is now nearly nine. Debris from the storm is strewn across the street. It is still dark, inside and outside the buildings. The streetlights aren't working. I drive back to the house, feeling anxious and hungry.

We don't know what to do so we huddle by the fire, trying to reassure ourselves that we must be mistaken about the time. We toast bread and crunch it dry. Time passes. We boil water ready for tea to welcome the estate agent, but no one comes.

In due course, we hear the village clock strike twelve noon. The sound drifts across the moonlit fields and lanes, as the wind gently stirs the leaves in the garden.

Between Jo Gatford, Cindy George, and Mark Taylor, this volume represents a reunion of sorts for authors who appeared in our 2014 anthology There Was Once a Place. *At least, I assume they're the same authors as before. One can never be entirely sure, after all.*

The Double

Mark Taylor

She woke up on a sofa, as she so often did when waking was this painful. Four miles away, her other self slept soundly in her bed.

She closed her eyes against the unwelcome daylight and felt it reaching behind her eyeball like a crochet hook. Her mouth tasted stale and sour, and would never be moist again. The pain in her back might have been the way she had slept, or some object she had been lying on, or an unnoticed injury.

Jasmine had a soft spot for hangovers. That feeling of being completely unable to turn the mind to anything except its own miserable experience: it was the nearest she ever came to meditation.

This morning, however, something interrupted her introspection: that bright daylight, and the pleasantly cool breeze that accompanied it, and the accompanying observation that this was not her sofa, nor the sofa of anyone she knew, and in some sense was no longer anybody's sofa, having been fly-tipped on a grassy verge between a narrow road and a farmer's field. Which was reassuring as far as its slight dampness was concerned, but in no other respect.

Having sat bolt upright in spirit, while her body remained limply horizontal, Jasmine performed a quick survey of her situation. She was at least fully dressed, albeit in a dress that would scream 'walk of shame' on the trudge home. She had at some point changed into her flats, which would be useful. And most unlikely of all, she still had her bag, tucked safely under her head, and inside it ...

... someone else's wallet, someone else's phone, and therefore (presumably) someone else's blister plasters and paracetamol and makeup. Someone else had her exact bag – had probably bought it the week after she did, when it had gone half price and they wouldn't let her return it – and they had mixed them up. Perhaps Jasmine had asked this other woman's Siri to direct her home, and it had brought her to this abandoned sofa, where the other woman lived.

The phone was charged, but locked with a PIN. The part of her that would have waited out this hangover watching trashy mystery TV shows wondered if she might somehow guess the number.

Jasmine's phone PIN was the home phone number of an old school friend, the first number she had ever memorised. The line was disconnected now, and Cassie was long dead. Cassie, who could have done anything; who had bigger dreams at eleven years old than Jasmine had scraped together by thirty-three. Jasmine no longer knew if she had chosen it out of sentimentality or just to get some value out of the bit of her brain where it lived. Her email password was a string of expletives she thought it was funny to type into the family computer twenty years ago, and which she had never bothered to change. If both of those and everything in between were possibilities, where would you even start?

She keyed in 1234, just in case. Nothing.

* * *

When a few cars had passed, all going the same way, Jasmine began walking in the opposite direction: the early traffic on these roads was generally heading out of town.

Before long she reached the Duke of York, and her mental map resolved. Jasmine and her friends had been coming to the Duke of York since they were sixteen, whenever one of them wanted to pull. It was a terrible place to meet people, unless you wanted to buy meat from them, but a principle had been firmly established, more important than reality: it had ten thousand men. The walk from here was about an hour and a half, and she was irritated to realise that it would do her hangover good. At home she would shower and change and eat and watch whatever detective programme was on until the girl with her bag called the locked phone, or she was absolutely certain she could go out without throwing up.

* * *

At the end of her road she began walking more furtively, hoping to dodge the eyes of neighbours, hoping not to pass the postman on her drive. As she peered around the hedge to check for him, she saw instead the familiar and, in most other circumstances, comforting, shape of John Bone (always 'John Bone', to distinguish him from her brother John, and because it amused her and annoyed him). He was standing on her doorstep with the look of a man who has just rung a doorbell and is resisting the compulsion to pull out his phone for the brief wait that follows.

Jasmine watched, not wanting to make herself known — embarrassed, yes, but also delighted. You almost never got to see what people did while they were waiting for you to answer the door. Was there, perhaps, a gleam of anticipation in John Bone's eye? Did his phone remain in his pocket because he wanted to make a good impression when she answered, even after sixteen years of friendship? Was he fitting his face into the expression he wanted her to see when the door opened?

Just as Jasmine was wondering how long he would wait before giving up, her other self opened the door and pulled John Bone into a suffocating hug.

* * *

It is like the moment you realise there is no ground where you have planted your foot, when time seems to stretch out but you cannot use it to think or act. There is too much feeling, and too much of it contradictory, to fit into an instant. It is as though she has split into a dozen copies, and feels for all of them at once. One Jasmine is astonished at this impossibility, while another is certain of a rational explanation. One is sick with anxiety, while another feels a thrill that at last something is happening to her. One is curious, one furious. And at the doorstep, another Jasmine, whose feelings are completely inaccessible.

* * *

She concealed herself around the corner until John Bone and the other Jasmine set off towards the high street, then retrieved the spare key from the sole of a boot-shaped plant pot and let herself in. She might be still drunk, still dreaming, or completely mad: whichever it was, the smart move was a shower and some sensible clothes.

The coffee table was just as she would have left it: cereal bowl drained of milk, her usual coffee cup with an inch or so left in the bottom, cigarette ash around the opening of an empty Diet Coke. She turned on the television to see Jessica Fletcher looking thoughtful, and turned it off again.

In the bathroom, her towel was already damp and another dress lay crumpled in the corner. In her bedroom, the other handbag sat on her bed, emptied of phone and wallet and keys. She opened the wardrobe for the more respectable of her morning-after outfits: the one she wore if she planned on leaving the house; the one with the stretchy jeans. But the other Jasmine had been wearing her stretchy jeans; her stretchy jeans had gone striding down the street with John Bone. She showered and dried, and dressed in unloved clothes that the other Jasmine wouldn't miss. She drank a coffee and left the mug back on the coffee table with an inch left cooling in the bottom. She stuffed the dress she had taken off into the handbag she had woken up with, rooted through coat pockets for any paper money, took a Diet Coke for the road, and left. She kept the spare key — would keep it always, but never use it again.

* * *

The good café was a calm and a comfort, a light in the darkness and a cool refuge in the heat. The menu always had exactly what you needed and the staff sensed exactly the level of chattiness your mood required. All would be well in the good café. All would be well for John Bone and the other Jasmine, who would certainly be there now, eating the spicy breakfast hash that cured all hangovers.

Our Jasmine sat in the back corner of the bad café and looked through the wallet. Bank cards in the name of Miss Jodie Spencer; a National Insurance card, kept inexplicably safe; loyalty cards and cash and stamps. On the driving licence her own face, six years younger; that unfamiliar name; her parents' old address; her date of birth.

Seized by a sudden thought, she slipped into the toilet and looked into the mirror. There she was, just as she had always been: not transformed into someone else; not even six years younger with bad hair to match the old photograph. Jasmine was Jasmine was Jodie. She splashed cold water on her face, the way they do in films. It didn't help; it just made the collar of her T-shirt wet.

When she emerged from the toilet, Annie was sat at her table. Of all the failings of the bad café, perhaps the worst was that Annie inexplicably favoured it.

'I thought I recognised your bag!' said Annie brightly. 'You don't mind if I join you, do you?'

Such questions from Annie did not seek an answer, and Jasmine was happy not to give one. She mumbled something greeting-adjacent and sat.

'So lovely to run into you! It's been so long. Have you ordered?'

'No,' said Jasmine, 'I can't decide what I want.'

'Spoilt for choice in here, aren't you?' said Annie, absurdly. They settled on the full breakfast, and for once Jasmine was glad to have Annie steamrollering the decision for her.

'Are you okay, Jas?' Annie asked as they waited. 'You look worried.'

Jasmine felt her stomach turn and didn't know if it was the situation, the hangover, the café, or the company. She opened her mouth to say she was fine, worried that the coffee and Coke would come up. Instead, just as involuntary, came: 'I don't know what to do, Annie. I don't know what to do.'

Annie nodded slowly and put a hand on her shoulder. 'I get it, Jas. I totally get it. Nobody wanted to say but we've all been worried for a while. The job, the dates, the drink, the tearfests. And it's okay. You mustn't feel ashamed, and it's okay not to know what to do. You know you need to do something, and that's massive, it really is.'

Jasmine just stared at her.

* * *

They talked for an hour about Jasmine's spiralling life. She agreed to a GP visit, group therapy, meditation, mediation, exercise, hoping that each concession would be the one that got Annie to leave her alone. She had real problems to deal with now, problems that Annie couldn't hope to understand, and the last thing she needed was to fill her head with all this talking. But she played along, and as she did so, she thought: I can't stay here. I can't see any of these people ever again. I can't be me anymore. Which meant she could say anything. Which meant she could go anywhere.

When Annie left for spin class, Jasmine stood across the road from the good café and watched through the window. There was her other self, laughing with John Bone. She didn't look like everyone was worried about her. She didn't look like she didn't know what to do. She looked carefree in the company of her best friend. And there was John Bone, smiling too, and pouring her water, with that inscrutable look on his face that he always hid if he knew she was looking.

Jasmine pulled out the phone and tapped in Cassie's phone number. Behind the icons on the unlocked home screen was a view from the peak of a mountain she had never climbed: low sun spilling over a calm lake, and more world than she had ever seen in one place.

* * *

A decade later, Jodie sees John Bone in a cavernous secondhand bookshop. Time stretches again, giving her long enough to decide she should hide behind the poetry shelves, and to know that she is about to call out to him. Long enough to realise he is just John, now: there is no John Spencer, and Jodie values intimacy over amusement. Long enough to wonder if he and Jasmine have lost touch; if he grew tired of her selfishness and her unreliability and the walls around her heart. Long enough to construct an idea of how everything can fit together just right, and they can be friends again. Long enough to hope.

She wonders, as she often does, where her other self is at this moment. In the same old house, whose key she keeps on her keyring? In the Duke of York, starting early? She has looked up friends and family online, seen their new jobs and weddings and children and funerals, seen the good café close and the bad café prosper. But she never looks up Jasmine.

She calls out, and he turns.

Jacqueline Gabbitas is making her first Fiction Desk appearance with this eerie story, inspired by Japanese ghost stories but set in Scotland.

Run 44

Jacqueline Gabbitas

No one takes the Run but me. Bad luck, they call it. I don't know much about that; my luck's no worse, no better than most others. At the start, I didn't realise what the Run was — just another fare, simple and easy, tips always generous. No one told me anything.

'Ferran Grange Hotel, please.'

She was the first. Beautiful in a plain kind of way, though it's hard to judge through a rear-view mirror. What I see of them is a backward reflection in the dark; half a face, a pair of hands with a wallet or purse, a way of moving as they walk away. They rarely come back. Not to the cab, anyway.

She sat in the back. Quiet. Occasionally she looked at her hands, the back of my head; but mainly she stared out the window. She didn't once glance at the meter. They never do. They aren't all like that — quiet, I mean. People are different, after all. Even at such times. Some don't stop talking from the point they get in my cab to the point they get out. Some of them seem happy, I don't know why. These ones are the hardest to bear. When they get out I can't look them in the eye, just take the money, talk to the dashboard. They all look like my kid; she's only nine but they still look like her, even the old ones, even the blokes. Her name's Joozy. She brings me paintings from school every Tuesday. Tuesday's art-class day. She settled in to the new school just fine. We'd been here a month by the time I'd got this job, and she was missing her mum. Her mum had called her Juliette, a pretty name.

'I like your drawing,' the woman said. It was the first thing she said for at least twenty minutes.

'My daughter,' I said, smiling. 'She's a bairn. She likes painting.' I yammered on for about a minute. I thought the woman had wanted to talk but she just nodded, took a weird deep breath and pinched her lips together. Looked out the window. I didn't know any better. I let her be.

I pulled up outside the Ferran Grange Hotel, heard another weird breath behind me, but paid it no mind. The hotel had been impressive in its heyday. Station hotel off a branch line. Sea nearby, two cities. On the outskirts of nowhere, protected from the worries of the world. If you didn't know, you could probably do something with it like apartments or shops. It's not even used for storage now. The windows are boarded up except for the ones at the top and they're broken or missing. It'd been white, once. There was no graffiti anywhere, not even on the old stables. This surprised me, back then.

'Are you sure this is the place, hen?' The signage stood out in the brickwork: Ferran Grange Hotel. The woman looked at me. If I was to put an age to her, I'd say she was about twenty-eight. She was skinny. Her coat and jeans must've cost a bit; shoes, too. She had a handbag but it was more like a little backpack on strings. Joozy had one like it. Her mum bought it her before she got sick. My wife, that is, not Joozy.

The woman leaned towards the window, then looked up. Nodded.

'Okay, then,' I said. Or something like it. I remember telling her the price: £42.15. I expected that shocked little breath that comes with any fare past a tenner but it didn't come. I tried to clock her properly through the rear-view but it was dark and all I could see was the top of her head. There was the sound of a zip opening, paper rustling. Her hand passed three twenties through the hole. They were neatly folded as if they'd been prepared beforehand. With them a whiff of vanilla and rose musk. Joozy's mum wore musk. I fumbled in the coppers box next to the gear stick.

'Keep the change,' she said. Her voice was plain but beautiful as well. Younger than her face.

'No, hen, look that's nearly twenty quid.' It was too much. Mistakes are easy to make. She'd meant to give me a fiver, not a twenty.

'Keep the change,' she said again. Then she opened the door – I was too stunned to think to open it for her. I watched her leave. When she reached the door of the hotel, she took out her phone and made a call, turning left onto a path that wound around the building. As I put the car into gear I saw a woman and a man in one of the top windows, waving. The light behind them a weird green. Ah, she must have been meeting them. That's what I told myself. Then I drove off feeling giddy for the tip, and checked in for the next fare.

'Everything okay?' The voice was crackly and breaking up, so I couldn't be sure if it was Sandy or Ella on the desk. It should have been Sandy, but it sounded high like a girl's, so Ella, then.

'Peachy, hen,' I said. I remember turning onto the main road when I heard: 'Who you calling "hen"?' It was Sandy, clear as day. I think I fumbled some words. All the man said was: 'Green Bar, Ranger Street. Pick up Gordon. Going to 56 Montgomery Place, West Side.' Sandy was a humourless soul. I asked about Ella. He said this was his shift.

* * *

It took me a while to work it all out. Four fares. All Sundays. I pried it out of Ella, and Eddie and Tommo backed her up. They two never did the Run anymore. Bad luck. I tried to make Sandy call the police, tell them what was happening but all he said was, 'Aye, and this is what they'd say: "Can you prove it? Have they said anything to suggest they's was gonna kill the'selves? There might be any reason they have for ganning to Ferran Grange."' He said it like he'd heard it said before. Tommo sussed it right off; said his first time he'd turned the cab around and had to drag the fare out back in town because he wouldn't leave. The man just left a shitty review online then walked onto the railway tracks the next night. I thought about that. There's something about trains on tracks that sounds like the lullabies Joozy's mum used to sing.

Then Christmas. New Year's. After that first holiday, I swore I wouldn't do the Run again. Seven fares. I couldn't help a one of them back then. But Ella says I have a quiet voice for a cabby, calm. Caring for a dying woman does that to the way you speak. So, sometimes, on the Run I can talk to the fares; sometimes we don't even get half-way to Ferran Grange before I turn around. I wait with them until someone comes — paramedics, family. Sandy never docks the waiting time; this still surprises me, even now. But that first New Year's. There was a guy. Built like a shithouse. Tall. When I opened my mouth he told me to shut my fucking hole. He thumped the back of my seat and we almost both ended up dead before we even reached the hotel. I shut my hole. Kept it shut. He calmed down the closer we got to his destination.

'£12.30, pal,' I said. He gave me £20. Didn't even look at it.

'Fucking pal,' he said. Got out.

I didn't hang around. Pulled the car round to the right; this way I didn't ever have to see the top windows. I mean, why didn't anyone tell me about the windows at least? A week after that very first fare, I'd gone back, this time with an old guy smelling of menthol who couldn't stop coughing. In one of the windows was the skinny twenty-eight-year-old woman. The light behind her that same weird green — made her sort of see through. She wasn't looking at anything particular but she watched the old man shuffle up the path and waved to him like she knew him. I drove off, banked the corner of Gerrid Street about a quarter mile away, then phoned Sandy to call it in. 'Okay,' was all he said.

There are too many familiar faces now.

* * *

I don't know why they do it. Not the dying, that's none of my business, but why they come all the way out to this place. Jumping's a gruesome death and I still don't get what the police around here are up to. I mean, what happens to the bodies?

They always book, the fares; never standing on the street, never flagging me down. And I've not once seen any other cabs near the place. I asked Ella way back if other companies took these bookings, but she just shrugged and gave Sandy a weird, sort of knowing, look. There's a story there, I bet ten to a dollar there is.

It's Christmas next week. Going to be a white one, they say.

* * *

'Grae? Grae? We've a Run 44. Name o' Morrisman. Pick up 132 Arbour Road.' Sandy calling one in. I'm five minutes away. 'Right,' I say. I always say 'Right'.

Morrisman. 132. Nice house: cream painted walls, double glazing, cat flap, double garage, garland wreath on the door. Even has one of those American mailboxes you see on the TV. Out of place here. The door opens and the Christmas wreath flaps around — someone should get that fastened down. A woman steps out and makes sure she locks the door behind her. She's wearing a blue coat and trousers — a lot of them wear blue — and red gloves and hat. Hardly any wear red.

She gets in, smiling.

'Hello,' she says. 'Is this okay?' She sits up front, which is rare but not an issue. Her perfume has ginger in it, ginger and some sort of flower.

'No problem,' I say. She asks for some music on the radio. Christmas carols sing out.

'Aah.' She seems happy with that. I don't say anything until she says: 'Is that Ganesha?'

'Yes,' I have to say, because it is. Not many people see it from the back of the cab, tucked up on the sun visor. 'My daughter drew it. She's ten next month.'

Morrisman (Miss or Mrs, I don't know which) nods. 'My sons used to draw me robots,' she said.

'Yeah?'

'A-huh. Your daughter's good. Why Ganesha?'

'Her mum,' I say. We talk a bit about the elephant god. About Joozy. My wife. She nods a lot, has a soft voice. Christmas songs playing, Ganesha smiling.

I ask her: 'Why robots?'

'My laddies build them,' she says, 'enter them in fights.'

I have to laugh at this. 'What, Robot Wars?' She laughs, too.

We turn off the main road. She straightens the gloves on her lap, strokes the soft wool. The road's easy tonight, gritted.

She tells me about her husband. This time last year. Slipped on ice. Aneurism. The jolly music on the radio breaks up so I turn it off; there's always interference when we get up close. The hotel is there. She gets out.

'Here you are,' she hands over the money, her voice pinched in. 'Happy birthday to your bairn.' She walks up the path. I mind how she goes. When she reaches the door, she turns and looks at me. Something, something there. I drop the engine. Phone in.

'I'm hanging on a bit, Sandy. Not long.' He can't hear me because of the static, but he knows. 'Nae problem,' he says through the crackling of the radio. 'Nae problem.'

I turn the radio on, the white noise some comfort, and every so often a voice comes through, ordinary, alive: talking about turkey and trimmings, church services; that kind of stuff.

Given the success of his award-winning children's fiction, we're fortunate that Alastair Chisholm still finds the time to provide us with his excellent short stories. Hopefully he won't burn out – maybe he should spend more time relaxing in the garden.

earth

Alastair Chisholm

The grass was worried. He sensed it as soon as he awoke, heard the long thin strands shivering and trembling. *Something coming*, it whispered. *Something bad.*

But grass was always fearful, scared of every little thing. He lay in his bunk and listened for a while longer, feeling the sunlight warm against his eyelids. Apart from the faint buzz of insects, it was quiet.

The grass whispered again, and he sighed.

'Yes, all right,' he muttered. 'I'm coming.'

He climbed out of his bunk, pulled on a pair of tattered leggings and wandered into the kitchen. He drank half a glass of water and poured the rest into a little tray of seedlings on the windowsill. They were doing well, he thought. Some were already uncurling, showing tiny pale orange leaves.

He stretched, scratched the grey stubble on his chin (no, not grey, he admitted with a smile: white now, and white hair too, over a walnut brown face), and looked out onto the garden.

It was early summer, and everywhere the flowers were opening, colours glorious in the morning sun. Bees flitted between yellow roses and philadelphus and sweet peas, and purple zimmer insects crawled over the Landfall plants, the freefalls and daisylikes and the golden promises. It was already warm, though dew was still on the grass, and their scents swept into the cabin on a light breeze. On two sides, rocky outcrops made natural walls that reflected the sunshine, creating a tiny microclimate that basked in warmth. High above him, wispy clouds decorated a deep blue sky.

'Beautiful day,' he said to Martha, as he made breakfast. 'Going to be a scorcher.' He took his bowl out onto the veranda and ate slowly, ripe strawberries and chorange slices, looking out.

'The clematis is getting a bit overrun. I'll sort that out today.' He sniffed. 'And the gzorts have turned, starting to rot I think; time to clear them out.'

Yes, a beautiful day.

'Makes you glad to be alive, eh?'

After breakfast he put on his old wide-brimmed hat and spent the morning tidying the clematis, and dead-heading the roses and dahlias, and composting the gzorts, the little Landfall pitcher plants full of sweet, sticky liquid that attracted and then ate parasites. In between, he tried to calm the grass, crouching to stroke it with the tips of his fingers, murmuring comforting nonsense.

Mid-morning, he stopped and nodded.

'Yes. Time for a break.'

Filling his bottle from the rain barrel, he wandered to the middle of the garden, where a small hill rose a metre or so. A tree stood atop the hill, next to a gravestone. The tree was thick with curling branches and large leaves, and he breathed a sigh of relief as he entered its shade. His eyes flicked to the gravestone and he smiled.

'Yes, yes, take it easy, I know.' He shrugged. 'You try telling the garden that.'

He sat and drew his hat over his brow and let himself snooze, with the bark rough and comforting behind him. These days he slept often, but in short spells; when he awoke after a few minutes he felt better. Standing, he placed one hand against the trunk for a few seconds, then frowned and reached up, and carefully pulled down a thin branch to peer at its leaves.

'Hmm,' he muttered. 'Looking pale. Not enough nutrients, I think.'

He was still frowning as he left the shelter of the tree, but then he stopped and looked up. He heard the grass again, agitated and nervous, and the sweet peas and crewels too. Even the smaller acers were trembling. Something was wrong.

He rasped a hand across his face and nodded. 'Well, then. Let's see.'

He walked out of the garden through a gap in the hedge, letting his hands drift over the plants and flowers. 'It's okay,' he murmured as he passed. 'Everything's fine.' But he knew it wasn't. He felt it just as they did, and as he turned into the north field, he saw the woman.

She wore black, stark against the azure sky and the bright pinks and yellows of the surrounding flowers, like a jagged hole cut out of the world. Her jacket was old and patched and re-patched with rabbit fur and hessian, but her boots were solid, with thick soles. A pack hung from her left shoulder, containing a canister of defoliant and a sprayer, and slung low about her waist was a gun, in its holster. She was smoking a cigarette, holding it in her left hand. The right hand stayed near her gun.

She was standing by a clump of puffers, peering into their beautiful, globe-like flowers, and at first he thought she was smelling their scent. But then she sucked on her cigarette, held the smoke for a moment, and blew it into one of the globes. It curled up instantly with a sound like a crumple of paper, and turned a dirty grey. The bush was dotted with other grey crumpled globes, half destroyed.

He swallowed his anger and waited for the trembling to fade from his arms. Then he said mildly, 'They don't like that.'

She grinned, and turned to face him.

She was young enough to make him feel ancient. Her hair was short and black, her face sunburned. An old scar ran from the top of her left cheek, across the nose, and above her right eye. Her eyes were blue and seemed to mock him.

'Howdy,' she said.

'They don't like it,' he said again. 'It kills them.'

She shrugged. 'They grow back, don't they?' She spat. 'They always grow back.'

He said nothing.

'This your place?'

He nodded. She flicked the cigarette away and picked a piece from her teeth. Then she stepped forward and held her hand out.

'Kali,' she said.

He shook her hand. She was strong, and she crushed his fingers in her grasp, held him until he winced, and then laughed. 'Silent type, eh?'

He shrugged.

'I was heading past,' she said. 'Saw your place. Thought maybe I could buy something to eat.'

He stared at the damaged puffer bush, and her gun, and the ground. Then he sighed and nodded.

'This way,' he said.

She whistled when they entered the garden. 'Hey, this is a real nice place you've got here.' She glanced at the flowers and shrubs in the borders, the soft shivering grasses, the gladioli and glowlights and dahlias competing to throw up the best colour, the most fantastic shapes.

'You do this all by yourself?'

He didn't answer. When they reached the veranda he said, 'I'll bring you something out,' but she shook her head.

'I'll come in with you,' she said, casually. 'Maybe I can help.'

He nodded again, and she followed him inside. The cabin was cool and dark, and suddenly seemed very small; she stooped to go through the doorway and stood, watching him, as he fixed up two bowls.

'This is a nice cabin, too,' she said. 'Clean.' She noticed the seedling tray. 'What's that?'

'Sunrays,' he said. 'For the winter.' She frowned.

'You let local life into your house? How do you stop it taking over?'

He shrugged. 'It doesn't.'

She snorted. 'Yeah it frickin' does. I've been on trail for twenty days, I've had to burn a circle every night to sleep on. I knew a guy, he built his place on stilts. Two metres off the ground, thought he was safe. One night the creeping ivy came up and burrowed right through the stilts and his whole god-sucking house collapsed.' She grimaced. 'You can't trust it.'

'Here's food,' he said.

They ate on the veranda.

'What is this?' she asked, peering into the bowl. 'No rations?'

'It's salad. From the allotment. I grew it.'

'Yeah?' She held up a small, round fruit. 'What's this?'

'Tomato.'

She sniffed at it. 'Is it Earth?'

It took him a moment to understand what she meant. 'Yes. From Earth, yes.'

She bit into the ripe tomato, and seeds burst out into her mouth and down her chin. 'Ah!' she spluttered. Then: 'Tastes good! Tomato, eh? And this?'

'Cureberry. It's ... local.'

She spat that out. 'What the hell, man?'

'It's fine. It's not bad for you.' He sighed. 'Try the green things. They're edamame beans, good protein. They're Earth.'

But she was suspicious now. She poked through the bowl with her finger, searching. 'You got any meat?'

'No. Not for a long time.'

She nodded.

'Yeah. Not even rabbits these days. God-sucking plants. They eat them in their burrows, you know? Just wrap around 'em in their sleep, squeeze 'em to death.' She looked across the garden. 'You got a lot of locals here, old man. You want to watch out for that.'

She glared at them, then chuckled.

'Hey, you never told me your name.'

He actually had to think. 'Cam— Cameron,' he said at last.

'Cam-Cameron?' she repeated, in a mocking voice.

He shook his head. 'Cameron. My wife, she calls me Cam.'

The woman's smile faded, and her hand drifted to the gun belt. 'I thought you lived alone.'

He nodded, and waved out at the garden, towards the hill. 'My wife's there,' he said. She followed his gaze and saw the headstone, and the grave beneath it. Her face relaxed.

'Well ...' She shrugged. 'People die. How long?'

He tried to remember. 'Thirty years now, I guess.' He raised his eyebrows in surprise. 'Yes. Long time ago.'

'You been here thirty years on your own? Man, I'd have thought you'd be pleased to have company.' She threw her head back and laughed loudly. She seemed to take up all the space; black and raucous, confident, dominant. A canker rooting herself in the heart of the garden.

'You see many people? Anyone around nearby?' She spoke as if just passing time, letting her leg swing. Her eyes moved constantly and saw everything.

'No,' he said. 'There's no one near. Sometimes strangers.'

'How come you're not dead?' He frowned, and she gestured at some of the plants. 'Goddamned *locals*. How come they haven't eaten you alive?'

He shook his head, helplessly. 'They're not hostile. Just defensive. They think we're an invasive species. Really, they're semi-sentient, if you listen to them —'

'They're *plants*.'

'They're more than that. I've studied them; that's my job. I mean, that's what I was, before we came here —'

She leaned back. 'Wait, before what? Are you from Earth?'

He shrugged. 'Yes.'

'As in, a colonist?'

'... Yes.'

'Wow,' she said, looking at him in mock-respect. 'You must be the oldest guy I ever met.'

She pulled a flat metal box from her jacket and opened it to reveal three bedraggled cigarettes. She lit one herself, didn't offer the tin to Cam. She took a long drag and spat over the veranda, onto a clump of poppies. The grass shivered; he ignored it, but the woman's head whipped around and her hand moved, not for the gun, but to the sprayer in her pack. She pointed it towards the garden, waving it from side to side, and for a second, fear crossed her face.

'What the hell was that?'

He shook his head. 'Just the grass. It gets nervous.'

But she stood up and scowled. 'It goddamn should be,' she muttered. She clumped down the steps and peered at the grass as if it were lava. 'Local? This is local grass? It looks real.'

'It adapts. It grafts easily, creates hybrids. That's how the ecosystem works here, everything's interconnected.'

She shook her head. 'I don't know what the hell you're talking about.' She cautiously poked at it with the toe of one boot, and he almost laughed.

'It's harmless,' he said. 'Look.' He walked out onto the lawn, enjoying the prickle of short stems beneath his bare feet, towards the hill and Martha's grave. After a moment she followed him, still waving her sprayer.

'This place is weird,' she muttered. 'This isn't normal.'

She took another drag at her cigarette and blew the smoke out in a short harsh push. 'Why the hell would you want to come here? I was *born* here and I know it's a shit-hole.'

He thought back.

'It seemed like paradise,' he said at last. 'This world was so lush, so full of life. Martha, she was a gardener, and when she saw it ...' He smiled. 'I wasn't much of one, back then. I was a biochemist. But it was a chance to escape the mess on Earth, start again. A new Eden.

'But the Company destroyed it. Burning, and burning ... Martha, she grew sick of it. She begged me to leave the colony, so we took what seeds we had and found this place. She had an idea we could talk to the locals, make peace with them.' He smiled. 'She was always stubborn.'

They'd reached the shade of the tree, its arms waving gently above him, and he gazed at the rough stone that marked her grave.

'And she was right. Life on Landfall is different. The plants here ... They have personalities, they talk, they react. They can *feel* us. And they can be reasoned with; she found a way. We built the garden together.'

He turned. 'This place is special, you see?' His voice trembled. It was hopeless, of course, but he tried anyway. 'There's no war here. You don't have to fight. We can work together, all of us —'

But the woman was already looking away. She didn't see the garden, just the ground. She stood next to the tree, analysing the land in lines and battle formations and threats.

'Yeah, it's sweet,' she said. 'Lots of food, cover from the cliff walls, hidden away ... Bad visibility though. I mean ...' She smiled. 'You didn't see me coming, did you?'

He nodded, ruefully. 'The grass tried to warn me.'

'What?' Her eyes narrowed.

'This morning. When you were coming down from your camp on the hillside. The grass warned me.'

For a second she didn't react. Then she said, 'Is that right?' Her voice still sounded relaxed. 'The grass told you. How about that.' She finished her cigarette; threw it, still glowing, onto the ground.

'What else did the grass tell you, old man?'

'That you weren't alone. That your two friends were following.'

She nodded and looked away. Her lips pursed as if amused. Then she shrugged.

'Hey fellas!' she called over his shoulder. 'Out you come.'

He turned as two men emerged from behind the cabin, one on either side. They were dressed like her, rough jackets, dirty and patched, black like rot. They held their guns pointed towards him. When he turned back, the woman was holding her gun too, at her side.

She lifted her shoulders like an apology, and smiled. 'It's nothing personal.'

'I'm a person,' he said. 'You're a person. It's always personal.'

The smile fell away. 'Yeah, well. We need a place. We need food. That's how it goes. You got a good spot, here. Burn away the local life and this could be okay.'

'Please,' he tried. 'This is our home. It doesn't need to be like this. We can make the world *better* –'

But she raised her gun.

'We *are* making it better. We're making it *ours*. You're an old man, Cam. It's time for you to join your wife.'

He looked into the black circle of the gun barrel. For a moment he caught a scent on the air, of sweet peas, delicate and sharp, and the citrus tang of the philadelphus, and the rich warm loamy smell of the chorange plants. He felt the grass beneath his bare feet. The sun shone, dappled through the leaves of the tree, and he closed his eyes.

'She never left,' he murmured.

'Kali!' shouted one of the men. The woman's eyes flicked towards him. He was struggling against a thick cable of ivy that wrapped about his waist and was pulling him towards the hedge. 'Kali!'

'What the –'

'Shit!' The other man's legs were tangled in the long border grass that now turned and wound about him until he lost his balance. He fired his weapon into the tangle, with no effect. 'Shit! Help! Help –'

She spun back to stare at Cam. 'What's happening?' she snarled. 'You said this was safe! What's *happening?*'

He frowned. 'I'm sorry.' He turned his head. 'I can never watch this part.'

She lunged forward, raising her gun, but something whipped around her arm and grasped it tight. A thin curling tree branch, and another, and more reaching for her legs now.

'Stop this! Stop!'

He walked away from her, towards the north field.

'Stop!' Her hands were both caught. Desperately she tried to reach her sprayer, but more branches lifted her feet off the ground and dragged her back against the tree. She jerked with all her strength and twisted around, to see its trunk splitting apart, yawning like an open mouth, dark and dank and the smell of wet mouldy earth –

The trunk closed around her.

* * *

He stayed in the north field for a while, repairing the puffer bush as best he could, removing its burned globes and trimming the damaged stems. It was wounded, but not fatally, and he spoke to it as he worked and calmed it down.

By the time he returned to the garden there was nothing to be seen. The two men were barely visible, hillocks of grass and ivy that would soon melt back into the earth, and the grass was tranquil again. He climbed up to the tree and rested his hand against the trunk again, listened for a while, and nodded. He checked its leaves and smiled in satisfaction.

'There, my love,' he said. 'Better already, eh?'

He stretched, and sat. For a few seconds he contemplated his wife's grave, and the rough stone marker. Then he pulled his hat down, leant against her trunk and went to sleep.

*Cindy George's latest Fiction Desk story takes a look
at what our ghost stories and superstitions might have
to tell us about who we are and how we live.*

The Pirate's Grave

Cindy George

You run three times around the grave. You shout his name three times. And you have to do it at midnight.

I never did it of, course. I was very much not that sort of child. I was, it turned out, exactly the sort of child who'd grow up to become a parole officer, and that sort of personality isn't really compatible with running around churchyards at midnight summoning ghosts. Anyway, I thought being a kid in those days was scary enough already, thanks. It was dark all the time, everything viewed through a film of coalsmoke and the fumes from leaded fuel. Power cuts filling houses with darkness and silence for hours even when it wasn't a Sunday. Adults might as well have been aliens, but usually you'd be alright if you managed to guess what they wanted. I was terrified of everything from gorillas (which hardly ever troubled us in the West Midlands) to food with smiley faces on it, to the theme tune from Emmerdale Farm. You wouldn't catch me talking to ghosts, even if I'd had any friends to dare me.

'Guess what, Mingnut?'

Graham Borridge and his gang from the Other School used to talk to me on the way home sometimes. I'm still not sure if they were being friendly or if they just thought it was funny to pretend. I moved my haversack to the shoulder furthest away from Graham in case he tried to gob on my R.E. book again. You weren't allowed to complain when kids from the Other School did stuff like that, because apparently it wasn't their fault. You were supposed to count your blessings instead. Even the thickest of kids from the Other School could have confidently counted my blessings for me. It wasn't a very high number.

'Mingnut! Guess!'

'I don't know. You must have done something special. Did you have a wash this month?' I always said stuff like that. I must have thought it was clever when it was actually a very stupid way of asking for a dead arm or a wedgie. This time it was a foot hooked around my shin, sending me crashing haversack first into a rainbow puddle of oil on the tarmac. Graham was so eager to tell me his news that he immediately hauled me back up by the hood of my snorkel parka.

'You know our Waz?' he began, rhetorically. Everyone knew his brother Waz. Especially the police. 'He went to the pirate grave, on his own at midnight.'

Even if Graham hadn't been holding my face close to his by a fistful of moulting fur trim, this would have got my attention. I believed him instinctively and immediately. Anyone taking on this adventure would have to have an absolute disregard for the consequences of their actions. If that described anyone, it was Waz.

When I first started as a parole officer, I quickly learned that most of the people on the wrong side of my clipboard were confused as to how their lives had ended up here. They had only been doing what they needed to do. They'd only been doing what everyone else was doing. They'd only done what anyone would have done, in the circumstances. They thought they were the victims, and in many ways a lot of them were, victims of negligent or abusive families, of inadequate schooling, of bullying, racism, poor mental health management. A lot of them were, in my professional opinion, horrible little shits, but there was nearly always a reason why they were like that.

And then you had the ones like Waz. There weren't many of them. They were people who had absolutely no concept of cause and effect. They wanted to experience everything; good, bad, didn't matter, as long as it was something. They often ended up being druggies, but I did have one who'd simply walked into a school one day, announced she was from an agency, and taught soap operas and swearing for three weeks before anyone noticed there might be anything dodgy going on.

'It wasn't fair, just because I didn't have the GCSEs. They all think they're better than me. I know just as much as them. Who gave them the right?'

This was years ago, of course. I'd like to think she wouldn't be able to do that now. Last I heard of her, she was on the news again, campaigning to get nettle oil recognised as a cure for autism.

I was retired by then, and not missing work at all. I had plenty to do. Fridge always needs tidying and walks don't take themselves.

We used to go out for drinks once a week, when we'd finished our paperwork. I always looked forward to it, and then when I was settled in a sticky pub chair, slopping overchilled lager onto a used and swollen beermat and listening to Les's theories on immigration, I would spend the evening quietly looking forward to going home again. Sometimes I joined in the conversation, but I always seemed to get things slightly wrong, and Les would have to waste time explaining that it was alright for people like me, but people like him had to look after themselves. I never found out what he meant when he said people like me. I never met any.

The people who live round here are alright. They're not like me, but they're not like Les, either. Sometimes on my walks I worry that there's a chance of running into someone who might want me to stop and chat about the weather or the shortcomings of the binmen. If I think too much about chatting, I usually stay at home instead and watch the telly. I've got all the channels now, I can watch things whenever I like. It's a lot better than when everything shut down at eleven o'clock and then you'd be alone with yourself till morning.

Funny how I never used to like being on my own. I much prefer it now. I think it's a lifetime of other people that's done that. Probably starting with Graham Borridge.

'The ghost came right up out of the grave and said he was going to cut Waz's head off with his cutlery.'

'Cutlass?'

'Whatever. Something sharp, anyway. But then he told Waz that if he mended his ways he wouldn't hurt him. So Waz told him to —'

I never found out what, because Graham's friend Spod hit me over the back of the head with my own bendy ruler that he'd nicked out of my haversack, and they all ran off.

It's funny how I remember all that, but I have trouble remembering to get the bins out on the right day ever since they changed it three years ago. It's not like I saw much of any of them after that. Graham and Spod fell out over a recorded-over cassette tape, and they weren't quite so keen to bother me individually. I never heard any other parole officers talk about either of them, so it's just possible they did alright.

Waz disappeared before his O levels and everyone thought he was in prison, but in the nineties he turned up in Ghana, covered in tattoos and making headlines for the outstanding results of his maverick approach to improving education provision for rural children. He's got an MBE now. I'd never have imagined he'd even be able to spell MBE.

And I passed my exams and got a job. I wanted to help people. I don't know why, because it's not as if people had ever done anything for me. I was good at it, though. Sometimes I'd have a laugh with my clients, but they still did what I said, more often than not. I talked to all sorts of people every day, the nice but misguided ones, the insufferable ones, the desperate ones, the cheerfully bad ones, and Les. Eventually, I think I just ran out of things to say. I wonder when I last had a laugh?

My evening walk was getting later and later. I wanted to avoid the dog walkers, all reluctantly closing the front doors behind them after dinner with their resigned expressions and their poo bags. They always cheered up if I said what a lovely little terrier Charlie was, as if his appeal was all down to them. Then I wanted to dodge the night shift workers. It was an easy walk to the supermarket or the hospital, especially when they were used to being on their feet all night, they said. Mainly the old ones. I didn't see any of them if I left after eleven. Trouble was, that was just in time for the pubs to be shutting. If there's one thing worse than chatting, it's chatting to a drunk person. It's always either the government or aliens with them. Eventually I was setting off on my walk about half past eleven, so that by the time I got to the end of the road, everyone had cleared off.

And that's how I found myself walking past the church one night at five to midnight.

I'm not sure how we all even knew about the grave. It didn't say anything about pirates on it. It didn't say anything at all. You could tell it once had letters on, but the stone had flaked away. I remember thinking it must have been at least a hundred years old, but now that I looked at it with adult eyes, it was obviously much older than that. I was fairly sure that no pirate had ever been buried there, as far from the sea as you can get. I wondered who was really under the stone, and what happened when they were woken. If I dared, would I be dragged into death by the jealous corpse of a seafarer who'd been banished to the Midlands canal system by an ancient curse? Or would I be like Waz, frightened out of my old life altogether?

Plenty of people run at my age, and I'm proud of them, but it's not for me. I can manage a sort of creaky trot that's probably slower than walking, but I felt it would be against the spirit of the thing to powerwalk around someone's last resting place. So round I trotted, as the old clock touched hands, and I shouted the name that the gravestone never said, but that generations of children knew. As I did it, I felt both unutterably stupid but also somehow scared, as if I was calling back the dark nights of smog and candles and nothing on telly, nights with no one to talk to you but the ghosts.

There are no ghosts of course, not even pirates. I did see a flash, as if the moonlight was reflecting bleached bones and a rusty cutlass, but it was a cyclist passing on the pavement, just the other side of the churchyard wall. And the voice I heard was definitely not that of an ancient seafarer:

'Keep more civilised hours. Take dog treats with you. You can learn all sorts from the drunks and the binmen. Maybe look up some old friends.'

That very much had the ring of my own inner monologue, jolted into action by the fact that I had made a steady sequence of foolish decisions that had led me to this particular idiocy.

As I hauled myself back over the churchyard wall, I suddenly remembered that the results of carrying out the ritual were, according to playground lore, that the ghost would strike you dead on the spot. I think the playground got that wrong. I don't think that ghost wants the company.

And so to Devon, where Matt's latest Fiction Desk story looks at how we cope with absence – of the appropriate punctuation, among other things.

Farmers Market,
No Apostrophe

Matt Plass

Robin arrived at Bramble Cottage with a bootful of Waitrose shopping, and for the first week in her new home she avoided the village. In seven days she spoke to no one, but she made discoveries: Devon hills are unkind to fifty-eight-year-old knees. A ghastly internet connection feels like an opportunity to disconnect from the grind of urban life until you're shivering in early October, trying to Google airflow settings for your new (new to you) wood burner. And – surprise – the countryside is anything but peaceful: birds scream from their tiny pulpits; animals shout. Listen to the cattle: they don't low, they bellow. Sheep stand stupidly in the fields, bleating at the ground.

* * *

Robin couldn't plaster — you get a pro in for that — and she was bad with ladders, but she could sand, paint, and rehang a cupboard door. As she worked on the cottage, room by neglected room, she shared her discoveries aloud, enjoying James's amused reaction. This was why she'd come: to work clay in the mornings — the back bedroom would make a fine studio — and to chatter to her husband without interruption, without her daughter Maggie telling her to face reality, without having to endure the long-faced concern of her friends. Now's the time to do what *you* want, everyone said. Well, she wanted to talk to James, the way she always had. So.

* * *

Soil must be limed, according to her new garden book. What was lime ... a powder, a liquid? Pellets, apparently, delivered by Amazon in a box like a cereal carton. Robin scattered tiny white beads across the soil and worried for the birds who might mistake her lime for seeds. She imagined twisted shapes tumbling from the sky, broken swifts and starlings littering the lawn that formed the southern border of Bramble Cottage. That, she told James, would be her as far as the village was concerned: she'd be that new woman from up country what killed all the birds. Robin balanced the lime carton on her wooden gate. She'd always wanted a farmhouse gate and now she had one. Whoop-de-fucking-do. She leaned her forehead against the gatepost, the weight of everything she didn't know about gardens hanging from her neck.

'Dry summer, this year.'

Robin started; the carton toppled and she had to catch it. A man stood the other side of her gate, late-sixties, short and useful-looking in a jerkin and heavy boots, sandy hair escaping from under a woollen cap. He frowned at her little red Fiat, tucked against the hedgerow.

'I'm Robin.' She found a smile and — *good* — a firm voice. 'Pleased to meet you.'

His eyes never left her car. 'Same. Enjoy the weather while it lasts.'

Robin's 'You live nearby?' died behind her teeth as the man turned away.

'Come on, boy,' he shouted into the hedge, unwinding a red dog lead from his wrist. 'Home time.'

She watched him disappear around the bend in the lane. She never saw the dog.

That evening, as she battled the wood burner, the old man's comment about the weather came back to her. It hadn't been mere pleasantry. More a judgement on her little Fiat's suitability for country roads mired by winter rain. You may be fine now, he'd told her. But just you wait.

* * *

Day eight, and two cups of coffee before starting on the lounge. The prospect of the lounge nearly sent her back to bed. Every peelback of wallpaper would reveal fresh horror: mould scars, plaster that crumbled at her fingertips, ancient wiring like blind snakes writhing in the wall. As she rinsed her coffee pot, she tested alternative place names on James: Rising Damp Cottage, Taste Malfunction Cottage, What-Dipshit-Put-These-Electrics-In Cottage.

Change of plan. Her second coffee had used the last of the milk, and she couldn't face soggy wallpaper without the promise of a tea break. Her options were to drive six miles to the nearest petrol station, or walk half a mile to the village. Robin pulled on her Barbour rain mac, wishing she had something waterproof that was less *London-goes-country*. She patted her hair in the hall mirror. In the strict checks and balances of her mind, braving West Colton just about made up for putting off the lounge.

* * *

A march through light rain, passing stone houses strung along the road. The old school, the old mill, the old police house – glistening charms on an antique bracelet – probably all holiday homes now, resurrected each springtime, dying back when autumn came. She met no one on the pavement, but a stream of vehicles swept past her shoulder. Something was happening somewhere.

Downtown West Colton offered a newsagent's, between a Boutique for Discerning Ladies (closed) and a village hall with a hand-painted wooden sign. *Farmers Market*. No apostrophe.

'I think I'm alright for farmers,' she said to James.

A teenage girl in a shapeless hoodie lounged behind the newsagent's till. She took Robin's five pound note and scanned the carton of Ivy Farm milk, *Devon's Finest*, fishing Robin's change from the till one slow coin at a time.

'The milk's locally sourced, then,' Robin said, as the silence stretched out between them.

'Not really.' The girl didn't look up. 'Ivy Farm's on the other side of the valley.'

'Oh, right. I see.'

'I'm joking.' Her trap sprung, the girl raised her gaze: *Gotcha*, her eyes said. *Just 'cause I'm not from the city, doesn't make me dumb.*

While her coins were counted, Robin looked anywhere but at the girl. She tried to read the local demographic in the spread of newspapers under the counter. *Daily Mails, Expresses*. Old people and Tories. Old Tories. Give it a few years and she might be an old Tory. She'd be old, anyway. And she'd be —

'Bramble Cottage.'

A voice from behind Robin, a statement not a question from a large woman in a yellow mac, past retirement age, with a sponge-cake complexion and white bell-shaped hair, in her arms a miniature dog with protruding lower teeth.

'That's right.' Robin forced a smile. 'Moved in last week.'

The woman massaged the dog between its pointy ears. 'Plenty of garden for one person to manage.'

Wow. There it was.

Sooner than expected, and much more brazen. Now Robin would have to admit to a husband, housemate, or the sad lack thereof. She looked into the woman's eyes — mud-coloured, toneless — and considered the effect on her village reputation if she said what came to mind, which was, *Wind your neck in, bitch.*

Instead she said, 'I'm used to a city garden. Pots in a yard. But it's good to learn new things.'

The woman's lips twitched, as if someone had whispered a joke in her ear. 'Make them yourself?'

'I'm sorry?'

'The pots in your yard. You're a potter, aren't you?'

Ceramicist. Don't correct her. 'I work with clay, yes.'

'Then you should join us.' A new spark flickered in the mud-coloured eyes. 'Thursday evenings. We meet in the hall at seven. We have a potter like you, two painters, a weaver, a woman who makes things out of beach glass, and a battalion of crochet artists, of course.' Her dog let out a whine and she shifted it in her arms, as if repositioning a griping baby. 'I should go. Henry hates it when I natter. But do come on Thursday. We call ourselves the Crafty Coven. There'll be wine, and I can introduce you to the ladies.'

'Sounds wonderful.'

Robin watched the Liberty-Bell-shaped head leave the shop. She pictured a damp village hall. She pictured *the ladies* — large women in yellow macs holding little dogs, eager to show off their woven dreamcatchers, watercolour daubs, *things* made out of beach glass. Robin had never found a way to lie about other people's art. James said that made her ballsy and authentic. Not down here, it wouldn't. Down here it would brand her as cruel and possibly unhinged.

She turned to thank the shop assistant — fight rudeness with kindness, James always said — but the girl had a set of white earbuds in, the cord between her teeth as she spoke to someone in a low, exasperated tone. As Robin left the shop, something made her turn back, something her brain had registered seconds after her eyes. The girl spoke into the tiny mic in her mouth, but between the fingers of her right hand she rolled the other end of the cord, the jack plugged into nothing.

* * *

'Of course I'm not going.'

Robin perched on the sill of the kitchen window, the one spot in Bramble Cottage with a phone signal.

'Good idea, Mum.' Behind Maggie's voice came the thud of a pneumatic drill, the beep of a reversing truck. 'Be alone.'

'I'm not going just to satisfy their curiosity.'

'Who's they?'

'The Ladies of the Crafty Coven. The whole thing is odd. How did that woman know? I never mentioned my work to the estate agent.'

'Maybe a neighbour saw your wheel being unloaded. Village people gossip.'

'She didn't ask my name or offer hers. And she came in after me and left without buying anything. And the girl behind the till was so rude. Pretending to talk on the phone so she wouldn't have to engage me.'

'Maybe they're out to get you, Mum. Or, maybe you want an excuse to stay in your cabin in the wilderness. God forbid you should make friends in your new home.'

'I'm more likely to make enemies. I'll say something mean about someone's pastel landscape. The wine will be undrinkable, and if I take my own, I'll look like a wanker.'

'So do what the kids do and load up on gin before you go out.'

'Sage advice, Darling.' Robin wedged the phone into the crook of her neck, freeing her hands to open a bottle of bio-dynamic, sulphite-free Beaujolais. Yep, wanker.

'Dad would want you to go.'

Through Robin's window, the sky over the hilltops glowed pink in the gathering dusk. At some point, despite everything, she'd made friends with her new kitchen, with this view, with the glow of the pilot light above the stove and the glint of sun on flagstone. Tonight, she would drink a glass of wine and watch the sun go down. She'd call a truce with the wood burner. Wine, a hot bath with her book, then bed.

'So how is it down there?'

Robin had almost forgotten Maggie was on the line. 'Good. Different. You know they say the countryside is quiet, but if you actually listen to the animals –'

'You still talking to Dad?'

'It's not even been a year, Darling.'

'Well, just try and do it in your head?' Maggie sniffed. 'You'll look less mental.'

'*Less* mental?'

'You know what I mean. I have to get back to work. Loveyoubye.'

Robin dragged a chair over to the window. 'Oh dear,' she said, as she settled back to watch the light dissolve. 'Our daughter thinks I'm mental.'

Half a glass of Beaujolais later, she said, 'You don't, do you? You don't think I should go?'

* * *

The garden would not be allowed to triumph. Robin developed a system: place a basket at one end of a flower bed, weed until the basket is full, then break for hot tea. An overwhelming task broken down into logical, manageable chunks. She told James he should be proud.

It was almost fun. Once she'd trimmed back the more aggressive brambles, the flower bed proved to be shallow, the earth friable, and the weeds happy to yield to her trowel. She enjoyed the slow tide of order that spread from one end of the bed to the other as the weeds piled high in her basket, and she enjoyed the autumn sun on her cheek and the fat robin who stood on her garden wall, broadcasting his demands.

Logical, manageable chunks of time. That's how you got through a day.

'Hello, there.'

The woman in the yellow mac was leaning over Robin's gate.

'Hello!' Robin stabbed her trowel into the earth, pulling off her gloves as she walked up the path. The woman had her ugly little dog in her arms and Robin remembered the animal's name from their first meeting. 'And hello to you, Henry.'

'No, no, this is Claude.' The woman scratched the dog behind its head to make it look up. 'Henry was my husband. He passed three years ago.'

Robin felt a sting of sympathy, replaced by something colder. *Don't think we're about to bond over our dead men.*

'I'm Robin.' She stuck out a hand in greeting, a deliberately masculine gesture to wrongfoot the other woman. Childish, but so what?

'Jennifer.' The woman took Robin's hand in a firm, plump grip. Robin had a sudden memory of her own grandmother, a woman unable to lift a heavy box above her head, but capable of squeezing every last drop from a wet bedsheet before it went on the line.

Jennifer was staring past Robin's shoulder. 'So, Robin, why Bramble Cottage?'

Robin pulled up her sleeve to show a set of fresh scratches, tiny kitten-claw marks down her forearm. 'I guess because the buggers are everywhere.'

'I use a spray — shouldn't, but I do. No, I mean, why choose this house?'

This is where you tell me the last resident murdered his family with an axe. 'Maybe I like a challenge.'

Jennifer's smile put dimples in her cheeks. 'Oh no, this has always been a happy house.' She leaned in, as if to share a secret. 'I think you'll both be very happy here.'

The old goat was persistent; you had to give her that. Robin imagined wheeling out James's corpse on a trolley, pulling back the sheet. *'Want a picture for the Ladies?'* She was still rolling a response on her tongue when Jennifer said, 'Are you coming Thursday? Craft night?'

'I'm afraid I'm busy on Thursday.'

'What a pity.' Another dimpled smile. 'Robin, can I ask you a personal question?'

Can you ask any other kind?

'Was Bramble Cottage the first place you saw?'

'The only place, actually. One viewing. Offer accepted.'

Jennifer seemed pleased. She kissed Claude between his pointy ears. 'I should go.' But she didn't move. Careful not to bump Claude's head, she leaned over the gate to whisper. 'Please come on Thursday. There's something I can share with you.'

'You can't share it now?'

Warm breath brushed Robin's cheek. 'Come Thursday.'

* * *

The fucking wood burner. Maybe she should spend some of the life insurance on a new central heating system, assuming she decided to stay in this crumbling shack in the Village of the Strange. Maybe she should burn Bramble Cottage to the ground and build a multi-story car park, just to annoy the neighbours. The little vents in the burner were meant to let oxygen feed the flames, and the vents were wide open, so why wouldn't the iron bastard stay lit? James would know, but Robin and James weren't talking. She'd told him she wasn't going on Thursday, and he was sulking.

* * *

Today's game was titled, *If I was going to the stupid craft evening – which I'm not – which piece would I take for show and tell?*

She'd already wasted an hour in the back bedroom picking through straw-packed crates, deliberating over Iznik-inspired tiles and hand-cast stoneware rice bowls. Robin had been 'building inventory' all summer: James' euphemism for low sales. What she hadn't told her husband, had never found the right moment to own, was that by pure chance, James's declining health had coincided with a flurry in sales – a dinner service to Huston; six amphorae to a collector in Vienna — and in the feverish hours of the night, Robin's brain had indexed the two: as her sales went up, James's health would surely come down. Nonsense, she told herself the next morning, but later that day she switched off the eCommerce function on her site. It had stayed off ever since.

In the back bedroom of Bramble Cottage, Robin listened to the ticking of the old house. 'Can we just agree to disagree on this one?' she said.

In her head, silence.

'Don't be like that.'

Nothing.

A chill took Robin, as if she'd fallen through ice. 'Don't do that!'

Nothing.

She pulled at a crate so hard it flipped onto its side. She ignored the crack of breaking ceramic; it was the crate below she wanted.

* * *

The earthenware vase sat on the kitchen table, beside a bottle of bio-dynamic Gamay. In any Soho gallery, the uneven walls of the vase would be taken as an homage to the Japanese wabi-sabi style. Down here it might just be badly made.

'You win,' she told James, as she packed the vase in newspaper. 'But don't do that again.'

* * *

Surprise number one: the interior of West Colton Village Hall sparkled. Strings of fairy lights hung like wisteria from timber beams, and wall-mounted heaters rained warmth upon a circle of folding chairs. Robin, dressed for damp, unwound her scarf as she stepped across the threshold.

Surprise number two: the Ladies of the Crafty Coven were not all well-padded, bake-sale types. Neither were they all ladies. Robin counted three men and nine women, including Jennifer who beckoned her over from across the hall. The youngest woman, clad in sleek yoga apparel, couldn't have been more than sixteen, the oldest no less than eighty, and — should this have come as such a surprise? — four of the twelve were not white. Robin recognized the woman who'd served her in the newsagent's, earbuds still lodged in her ears, and the stubby gent who'd appeared at her gate to glare at her Fiat. He had his back to Robin as he arranged wine bottles on a trestle table, but she knew him by the red dog lead wrapped around his wrist.

'You came.' Jennifer steered Robin toward the trestle. 'I'm so glad.'

Robin lifted her tote bag. 'Vino.'

'Add it to the stockpile. We're not exactly the Temperance Society. Now, Robin ... I hope wine isn't the only thing you brought along tonight.'

'Yes, well. A vase.'

'Can't wait.' Jennifer selected a bottle of red with a cartoon pig on the label. 'Can I tempt you?'

Not with that. But she let Jennifer pour her a glass. 'When you visited the house, you said you'd share something with me.'

Jennifer pressed her hand against her chest. 'I'm so glad you came.'

'Ladies, gentlemen,' a tall, stooped man called out, in a voice too deep for his narrow chest. 'It's eight o'clock. Shall we?'

* * *

They formed a circle on the folding chairs. Robin's visit meant introductions, a blur of names she wouldn't remember. By the time they completed the circuit, her jaw ached from smiling, and her glass of Rioja — supermarket smooth, but blessedly alcoholic — was almost empty. In her head, she told James she'd stay for fifteen minutes then make her excuses.

The last member to introduce herself was seated on Robin's left. She spoke with a soft, Midlands accent. 'I'm Pritta Khatri. Pritta the Knitter — that's what my wife called me. Drove her mad finding half-finished work around the house. I used to hide my wool under the cushions. I still do.'

Across the circle from Robin, Jennifer rubbed her finger and thumb together. 'Last week at the market, Pritta sold eight scarves. Eighty quid in two hours!'

'Ninety.' Pritta winked at Robin. 'I sold a bobble hat, too.'

'How wonderful.' Robin decided not to mention that her Vienna-bound amphorae had netted a touch over four thousand pounds. She realised that the circle was waiting for her to say something else. 'I'm Robin. I just moved into Bramble Cottage, the one with the wonky chimney stack. It's lovely to meet you.'

'We're glad you found us,' the tall man said.

'I hear you're a potter.' The young woman in the yoga top had an edge to her voice; no doubt the Lidl bag between her feet contained a ceramic something. 'What did you bring?'

'Come on Suze,' Jennifer said. 'We can't ask the new girl to go first.'

'I don't mind.' Robin pulled her tote into her lap and unwrapped the earthenware vase. The glow from the overhead heaters set tiny orange fires in the milky glaze. 'It's a vase. For bluebells.'

'Oh,' Jennifer said.

'The imperfections are deliberate. It's a style called wabi-sabi.'

Wabi-sorry, is how James had described her early efforts. His jokes could sting — she wouldn't pretend otherwise — but they pushed her toward perfection. This vase had been the first of many to turn out well. She offered it to Pritta. 'Do we pass things around?'

Pritta withdrew her hands. 'Not to Mrs Clumsy-Clogs.'

'It's stronger than it looks. Ticks both William Morris boxes.'

Pritta gave her a vague shake of the head. The girl with the earbuds said in a bored voice, 'The designer. The wallpaper guy.'

'That's him.' Robin ran a finger under the rough base of the vase. 'Morris said you should have nothing in your home that is not beautiful or useful.' She looked around the circle for confirmation and met a silence that she felt herself slowly falling into. 'My husband used to joke that I was a William Morris fantasy. Beautiful and useful.'

Where the Hell had that come from?

Then, she heard herself say, 'He stopped making that joke after a while. He told me it no longer felt right — it was chauvinistic, elevating looks over character. He thought I'd be pleased, but all I could think was that he stopped saying it because the beautiful part was no longer true.'

Christ, Robin. One glass of wine; she couldn't blame the alcohol. Around the circle, several heads were bowed. She'd embarrassed them.

But apparently, she hadn't finished. 'James could be difficult.' The words escaped before Robin could stop them. 'No one else saw it. He was a lovely man, and I loved him, but he could be cruel. And if he didn't get his own way, he'd sulk like a child.'

Prickly heat spread across her cheeks. She pressed her lips together, afraid now of her own tongue. She re-wrapped her vase in newspaper and put it back in her tote. The chairs were arranged so that she couldn't leave without breaking the circle. If James was here, they'd have left anyway, and she'd have felt awful, but they'd have laughed in the car and, by the time they were home, Robin would have made peace with herself.

But James wasn't here. And she'd just betrayed him to twelve strangers.

'Husbands,' Jennifer said. 'Difficult by design.'

'Wives aren't easy,' Pritta said. 'It doesn't make you miss them less.'

'I should go.' Robin tried to stand, but her legs were columns of water.

Jennifer held out both hands, as if she might reach across the circle to touch Robin's face. 'We know how you feel.'

The tall man nodded. 'That's why we're here.'

Spots of light pricked Robin's vision as twelve faces — twelve harvest moons — beamed back at her. Among them, Jennifer, the widow who referred to her husband in the present tense; Pritta-the-Knitter still hiding wool from a dead wife; the newsagent's girl who talked into a headset that wasn't plugged in; a man with a dog lead and no bloody dog. Robin could go around the circle and every one of these grinning waxworks would have a ghost at its shoulder. This wasn't a craft evening, it was a séance.

'I know what you're thinking.' The tall man lifted a finger. 'But there are no ghosts here, except the ones we make ourselves.'

The girl with the earbuds sighed. 'We know they're dead, is what he means. Nothing spooky.'

'Nothing, Christine?' Jennifer frowned. 'People find us when they need to, don't they?'

'Whatever.'

'Did chance bring you here from Penzance? Or Pritta from Nottingham?'

'What is this?' Robin pushed up onto her feet. She crushed the tote bag against her chest and felt the wall of her vase give with a silent crack.

'Don't be frightened.' Jennifer raised both palms. 'It's never easy to start the conversation. Please, sit down.'

'I don't want to.'

'Your call,' the girl with the earbuds said. 'But make up your mind. We can't do our thing until you do.'

'Christine, please.' Jennifer was on her feet. 'Robin, honey, let me tell you something you already know. When you lost your James, you were given space. You were allowed to wail, to hide away, to bulldoze through, whatever you needed to survive. But after a while, someone who loves you told you it was time to move on. Am I right?'

In the purple shadows of the beamed ceiling Robin saw her daughter Maggie, the thin mouth moving over a cup of tea in the Marks and Spencer café. Not just Maggie, all of them: doctors, friends — at different times, in different ways, using different words to say the same thing.

'Everyone's an expert when it comes to other people's grief.' The tall man's voice brought Robin back into the circle. 'And the experts tell us that moving on is healthy. They're right, of course. But there are more important things than being right.'

'We choose not to move on,' Jennifer said, her face tilted to the light.

Metal chair legs scraped on polished wood as the soft part of Robin's knees struck the edge of her seat. This wasn't a séance. This was self-help gone bat-shit crazy, and these people were insane.

'Christine's right,' Jennifer said. 'It's your call. But we hope you stay. There's nothing sinister, here. We meet, drink wine, and share our questionable crafting. We speak freely and without fear of judgement, to those who are in the room, and to those who aren't. That's all.'

Heat rained down on the crown of Robin's head. She closed her eyes and there was James, leaning against the wall of a crumbling barn somewhere green and quiet. He smiled at her, shielding his eyes from the sun. She asked him, *What do you want me to do?* But he just kept smiling in that irritating way he had when he was waiting for her to figure something out for herself. She heard Maggie's voice in chorus with her friends: the promise of new horizons, diminished pain. She reached for her husband through liquid sunlight. *Tell me. Tell me this is what you want for me.* This time, when James didn't answer, Robin knew why. He wanted her to say it out loud.

About the Contributors

Alastair Chisholm writes short stories and children's books. His picture book *Inch and Grub* won the Scottish Book Trust Bookbug Prize and the Queen's Knickers Award, and his children's science fiction novel *Orion Lost* was nominated for the Carnegie Medal.

Alastair lives in Edinburgh with his wife, family, and a cat, and he thinks it's weird to refer to himself in the third person. He likes biscuits.

Sarah Dale lives and works in Nottingham. She did an MA in creative writing at Birkbeck University, London, and in recent years has been combining her experience as a psychologist with writing by running writing groups for well-being. She enjoys writing fiction, non-fiction and poetry and has had a number of pieces published.

Gavin Eyers is the author of two ghostly novels, *The Deceit Birds* and *The Garden of Longing*, as well as short stories that have appeared in anthologies. He enjoys reading — and writing — fiction inspired by nature, the countryside, and spooky old houses. He lives in London and is currently working on his third book.

Jacqueline Gabbitas is a short fiction writer and poet. Her poetry collections include *Mid Lands* (Hearing Eye), *Earthworks*, and *Small Grass* (Stonewood Press). Her stories and poems have been published in various magazines and anthologies including *Cleaver*, *Contemporary Fairytales*, *Poetry Review* and *The Forward Prize Anthology* (Faber & Faber). She has also appeared on BBC Radio 3's *The Verb*. She has received two Arts Council grants for her writing and is a Hawthornden Fellow. She is a mentor for Pen to Print, and host of *Unfeared*: a podcast of ghost stories written by women.

Jo Gatford writes flash disguised as poetry, poetry disguised as flash, and sometimes things that are even longer than a page. Her work has most recently been published in *The Forge*, *trampset*, *Pithead Chapel*, and *SmokeLong Quarterly*. She is the co-founder of @writers_hq and occasionally tweets about weird 17th century mermaid tiles at @jmgatford. She wants to live on your bookshelf.

Cindy George lives in Coventry, surrounded by cats and ghost stories. She has written teen romance, advertising campaigns, music reviews, and once won an award from the World Health Organisation for promoting health and public hygiene. She has been a copywriter, a journalist, an editor, and a teacher. She now writes poetry, fiction, and things that don't know what they are.

Alan Gray is a writer/psychologist born in Horden, County Durham. He holds an MSc in experimental psychology from the University of Oxford and lives in London. His stories have appeared in various print publications and online journals, and he is a City Writes competition winner.

Matt Plass lives on the edge of Dartmoor. He works in Ethics and Compliance, and writes short fiction in his spare time.

Mark Taylor lives in Manchester with his wife and son, where inbetween making up stories about toy diggers he occasionally finds the time to make up a story for grown-ups.

Ben Tufnell is a curator and writer based in London. His stories have been published by *Elsewhere*, *Litro*, *Lunate*, *Storgy*, and *The Write Launch*, and as chapbooks by Nightjar Press and The Aleph Press. His debut novel, *The North Shore*, will be published by Fleet (Little, Brown) in 2023.

For more information on the contributors
to this volume, please visit our website:

www.thefictiondesk.com/authors

Also Available

www.thefictiondesk.com